A THUG'S REVENGE

SHE WAS A THUG'S WEAKNESS 3

SANTANA

JESSICA WATKINS PRESENTS

ACKNOWLEDGMENTS

First, I would like to apologize for the wait between now and the last part of this series I completed. A series of unfortunate events occurred that completely obstructed my ability to fully dedicate myself to this book. Aside from intense writer's block, general distractions and me trying to start a new business for women entrepreneurs, I was also in and out of depression. That in itself is a silent killer of dreams and can throw most anyone off track. If you are here reading this despite the long wait, I want to say thank you for your unwavering support. Please understand that this is truly my passion but there are forces that I can't control.

To Carmen TheHairGenie, I love you so much. You were the first person to encourage me to write when I lost my job. Thank you for always being that supportive friend. Everybody needs someone like you.

I would like to give a special shout-out to my dear friend Jennifer Graham, (Authoress Ascension) for her continued support, encouragement and prayers. This girl inspires me and keeps me going.

To Bello/Jullisa, my boo and one of my biggest supporters, thank you for keeping me on point. Thank you for bullying me into finishing this book and for being here since day one of my career. I really appreciate you.

To Fatima, you know I had to shout you out. You are such a sweetheart and I appreciate you for supporting me since day one. Love you, boo.

To my publisher, thank you again for choosing to sign me. I knew since the day I read Secrets of a Side Bitch that you were somebody that I would love to be published under. I pray for your continued success.

To all my readers, I love you guys so much, even if we aren't connected via Facebook, I love you still, lol. I really appreciate you taking the time out of your day to read something from lil' ole me.

FOLLOW THE AUTHOR

Make sure you're following me on social media. I've heard I'm pretty entertaining.

Facebook:

Author Santana

Jasmine Jones

Reader's group on Facebook:

Author Santana's Reader's Group

Instagram:

Author Santana

Twitter:

@authorsantana

A QUICK LOOK AT WHERE WE LEFT OFF...

TRE

All I can say is Thank God, my bro was already in Detroit. I know him missing the birth of his daughter would've killed him. Jas did the right thing by telling me. I guess she really did have a heart. I was surprised Isabella didn't put us out of the delivery room, but I could tell she wasn't happy. She kept giving Jas the death stare. I watched the interaction between them the whole time, and something was definitely up.

The thing that had me in shock was that Jas and Isabella were related. Another fuckin' plot twist. I knew that Jas knew everything about everything. I knew she knew what I had done to and with Isabella. Then everything became that much clearer. All three of these muhfuckas was in on it. Damn, right under my nose. The only thing that didn't make sense was the fact that Chase and Jas didn't seem to know each other at all, but Isabella was definitely sneaky enough to make the plan work without them knowing each other.

All this time, my brother and the girl I loved were conspiring with the enemy against me. I knew from the beginning she had something to do with this. Now, Jas admittedly talking to Silas that night of the club shooting had put things in perspective. Damn. I got got. It all made sense now. Jas was tryna cuddle all close to me in the waiting room, but I wasn't havin' it. I pushed her off me and just left. I hated the fact that I had feelings for her. It would make killing her that much worse on my conscience.

I didn't speak to her for a few days. I was waiting until Isabella's shady ass was out the hospital and feeling a little better before I confronted the three musketeers about their involvement in this shit.

"You home?" I asked Jas when she answered.

"Yeah, but why haven't you been answering my calls?"

"We'll talk about that when I get there. Isabella and Chase there?"

"Yeah, they're still here. She's refusing to go back with him."

"Good, I'll be there soon," I said and hung up.

Twenty-minutes later, I was pulling up in her driveway.

I approached the door and rang the bell. She let me in and I noticed a weird look on her face. She looked nervous and kinda scared. Exactly how a guilty bitch should look.

"Where's the baby?" I asked my snake-ass brother who was at the table eating lunch.

"Sleep right now. What's good witchu bro?" He dapped me up.

"Nothin' much but all four of us need to rap right quick."

"Cool," he responded.

I saw Jas give Isabella another weird look.

"So, I know who's been setting me up this whole time," I started.

"Word, bro? Who?" Chase asked like he genuinely had no clue.

"Yep. You three sorry muhfuckas." They all had shocked expressions.

"Hol' up bro, I know you ain't serious." Chase drew back, even laughing a little.

I was serious, serious as the gun I pulled out of my waist on them. I pointed it at Jas.

"Hell yeah I am. When you couldn't set me up to go to prison, you got this snake-ass bitch involved to get my guard down, ain't that right, Jas?" I gritted my teeth as I spit venom toward her.

"You got it all wrong," Isabella chimed in.

"Nah, it all makes sense now. Y'all hoes are cousins. You had the most motive, the means and the manpower to make this shit happen. I always suspected you, but I doubted your involvement when my brother vouched for you. Now I know he only did that cuz he was in on it too." I paced the floor, wondering who to blast first.

I was only hesitating because of the baby in the back. I didn't want to take her parents from her, but something had to be done.

"Jas, just tell him," Isabella said.

"Don't do this okay," Jas said as she became choked up.

"Tell him the truth before you get us killed," she urged.

"Whatever it is you better tell me before I shoot yo ass!" I yelled as she sat there lookin' foolishly at the floor.

"Okay, damn. Isabella offered me money to date you, make you fall for me then leave. But that was it. I have texts to confirm. We weren't in on any plot to put you in jail though, Tre, I promise. It was simply to hurt your feelings like you did hers. But I swear to you that's it. If you kill us, I promise this won't stop cuz it's not us. You gotta believe me." She held out her phone and showed me a text thread confirming what she'd said.

I still didn't buy it.

"Bitch, this don't prove shit but it's nice to know that this whole time you've been playin' a nigga. So that's how you got this nice-ass crib huh? From a payoff from this bitch." I chuckled to hide my pain.

"What? No! I didn't even get the money from her because I told her I couldn't go through with it. The money I used to pay for this came from my lawsuit."

"Whatever, bitch," I spat.

I had heard enough. I was ready to shoot something.

"Tre, please listen to me. It's not us. I swear baby." She tried to come closer to me, but I shoved the shit out of her and she landed on the couch.

"She's not lying. She refused the money. She said she didn't want to hurt you." Isabella rolled her eyes as she spoke.

Then she continued, "I was mad at you still and yes I did plot to get your heart broken, but she said she couldn't go through with it. That's the truth. Chase and I argued about this very situation. He kept badgering me about being involved in the setup against you to put you in jail, but this was the only plot I had. We argued, and he choked me and almost killed me over you. That's why I ran away. That's why I'm even here now. Your brother had nothing to do with this and neither did we."

I cocked my gun, ready to shoot. I almost pulled the trigger when my phone finally rang. It was an unknown number.

"Hello?" I answered with the gun still pointed at Jas.

"Drew?!" I thought he was dead, but he was on the other end of my phone with news of who was really behind this shit.

I just knew he was about to confirm my suspicions and tell me it was the three rats sitting in front of me, but then he muttered a name that never even crossed my mind.

"It was Marcus. He's behind this."

I was taken all the way back.

"What? Are you sure?" I was so confused at this point.

"Yeah, the day he went to kill Silas, his last words were 'but you the one.' Their whole interaction said that Marcus is the one who hired him to set you up at the club and again to try and kill you. Marcus was disappointed that he didn't complete the job. Sorry, brother," he finished.

I just stood there in utter disbelief. I couldn't believe what I'd just heard. I couldn't wrap my head around it. I dropped the phone to the floor and was snapped back into reality by faintly hearing Drew say "hello" over and over.

I grabbed my phone and called Marcus, but there was no answer. Then I went by my house, but he wasn't there. I thought long and hard about where he could be. Then a thought came to me which would explain exactly why he wanted me dead or in jail. Liyah must have told him about Ava and me. She had threatened me plenty, but I guess now she had all the motivation she needed to go through with it. I was so caught up in Jas that I didn't give a fuck about how Liyah was responding to the rejection she'd experienced from me.

Before this, I was so caught up in Isabella, I didn't notice how it affected Marcus when I started fuckin' wit' her behind his back. Damn! This whole time the answer was right in front of me, but I didn't even see it. I was really about to kill three people that weren't even involved. Thank God, I got that call in the nick of time. I wouldn't have been able to live with myself if I had taken three innocent lives. Well, two weren't all that innocent but they weren't responsible for this shit.

Since Marcus wasn't a resident of Michigan, I knew there was only a few places he could be, so I went to the casinos downtown and he wasn't there nor checked in at the hotels. Then it came to me. I sped onto the Lodge Freeway all the way to Southfield. I hastily made my way to Liyah's house. Lo and behold, Marcus' car was parked behind hers in the driveway of the house I bought her.

"Ain't this 'bout a bitch!" I exclaimed as I banged the steering wheel and sped away from the house.

If I didn't leave now and regroup, I was gonna murder my brother and that bitch and still be in prison. This needed to be premeditated. Any murder I did had to be.

I went straight home, showered and popped a couple pain pills cuz my head was throbbing after all the shit that happened today.

Soon as I got comfy, my doorbell rang. The earlier discovery had me on edge, so I grabbed my burner and went to the door. It was Liyah. I snatched the door open, my bare chest heaving up and down trying to suppress my need to kill this bitch right here. I peeped around for Marcus; he was known to pop out of nowhere. When he didn't show, I put my gun down and folded my arms, waiting for her to speak.

"So, you really chose her over me?" she asked like she didn't have a hand in trying to get me killed.

"You really got some nerve, Aaliyah." I shook my head, trying desperately to keep my composure.

"Me? You help to ruin my life and now you just throw me to the wolves over some new ass?"

This bitch looney as hell.

"You ruined your own life. Let yourself out." I told her, grabbed my gun and returned it to my waist, then walked away.

I heard her run toward me, attacking me from behind with a barrage of punches. I lost it. I quickly turned around and before I knew it, my hands were wrapped around her pencil-ass neck choking the life out of her. She clawed at my arms until she drew blood, and I finally released her. She collapsed to the floor gasping for air and coughing up spit as her eyes watered.

"Now get the fuck out my house!" I barked as I returned to my room.

I came back out minutes later to make sure she'd left. She was outside by her car being consoled by a couple of my nosy-ass neighbors. I scoffed as I closed the blinds and went back to bed.

~

The next day, I had been out running errands and plotting my next move in the situation. I had also gotten a letter that my pops would be released from prison in a week. That was the best news I could've gotten. Maybe my dad being out would help Marcus with his fuckin' issues. He always respected my dad if he didn't respect anyone else. In the meantime, I had been watching my back and looking over my shoulder all day, anticipating another attempt on my life from Marcus.

I had survived the whole day with no stray bullets coming toward me. As I made my way down my block, I noticed police cars, flashing lights and an ambulance. Maybe one of my old neighbors had fallen in the shower and life alert wasn't fast enough. I chuckled at the thought.

But as I got closer, I realized it was my house they were at. Caution tape revealed that it was indeed a dead person being brought out on that stretcher.

I parked and hopped out, running to the scene to find out what was going on at my house. I rushed to the EMT that was rolling a body out and tried to get answers.

"What happened here?" I asked frantically.

"Female victim found strangled in the master bedroom of this home," the female EMT said hesitantly.

"Who is it? Please let me see!" Then she unzipped the bag. It was Liyah.

I was approached by three officers.

"Are you Tre Carter?" one heavy set male officer asked.

"Yeah but..."

"You're under arrest for the murder of Aaliyah Carter. Put your hands behind your back," he told me as he began reading me my Miranda rights.

How the fuck did this happen? I didn't kill her. She was alive and well when she left. This time, my mind didn't need to even think about who did this. It was Marcus and with his expertise with murder, I knew for sure he could make this look like it was me. I was about to have a hard time getting out of this one. Even if I could gather evidence that it wasn't me, that would mean I would have to snitch on my own blood. God knows I couldn't and wouldn't do that.

"Nicely played, bro," I said to myself as the door to the cop car closed.

1

PRELUDE TO A MASSACRE

TRE

Ain't it crazy how the last time I told a story I was right here? Right in this stankin' ass prison, rotting away like some criminal scum? Every day I had to sit behind those bars, wrongfully, just added another bullet I was gonna put in my brother's head. I couldn't believe this nigga really framed me for murder over some pussy he got out the strip club. We were both young and dumb and made mistakes. That nigga wasn't perfect in the least. He was out here killing cats and dogs when we were kids. A straight up black Jeffrey Dahmer, but he wanna trip cuz I fucked a bitch of his that got naked for dollars? He should've been grateful I showed him these hoes couldn't be trusted, but leave it up to him to fall in love and betray his own flesh and blood over strip club pussy.

Now, I ain't trippin' too hard cuz I know I'm getting out of here. I wasn't even there when he planted her body or when she was murdered. The autopsy report came back, and she was killed at a warehouse. I was out and about at the time of death and my lawyer, the great and powerful David Steinberg was working overtime on them forensics. My dad was finally out of prison and he was working the hardest to get me out. Those two together, I knew I was as good as free. The only thing that held this whole process up was the DNA evidence under her fingernails where she had dug into my skin when I choked her out that night. All of that was taken into consideration and was drawing my release out longer than expected.

I was not about to waste another year in here again. I was willing to pay anybody, muhfuckin' DEA agents, the medical examiners, the judge, *whoever*, to get me out this bitch, post haste. I was literally dying in here. I wanted to see my baby, Jas so bad. I missed her like crazy. I wanted to apologize to my brother, Chase for almost killing him and his scudded-ass baby mama, Isabella. After learning she wasn't involved the way I thought, I knew I had to make amends for pulling a gun on them with their newborn baby only a few feet away. That was too savage, even for me.

Although I was still mad at Jas for being in Isabella's scheme to hurt me, I couldn't stop loving her if I tried. Y'all don't know heartache until you trapped in a prison cell after almost killing the woman you loved. Some people think death is the most painful experience but try being alive and well and still can't get to the person you want. Jas prolly hated me right now. She was prolly laid up under a new nigga, suckin' his dick and fuckin' him on the first night like she did me. I cringed just thinkin' about it.

She hadn't even written a nigga or accepted my phone calls. I kept trying to get Chase to contact her for me, but she wasn't havin' it. I didn't know what I was gonna have to do to get her back, but I was going to do whatever it took. It was no way in hell I was letting her go. I was letting nothing go. I had big plans for her and for my snake-ass brother...

JASMINE

Fuck Tre. Fuck his phone calls, fuck his letters, fuck his good-ass dick, and everything else. I was not gonna be the bitch forgiving him for his fucked-up outburst. This nigga put a *fucking gun* in my mouth because he thought I had something to do with all the shit that was happening to him. I had never been so hurt, angry, and scared in my life. He knew exactly what I went through after Monty tried to kill me so the only reason I could think of for him pulling that shit was that he was really gonna shoot me.

All that love shit went out the fuckin' window. There was no trust, there was no loyalty, no nothin'. This nigga didn't give a damn about me or my word. It meant nothing. My heart hurt every time I was forced to think about the day that this nigga almost blew my fuckin' brains out. Nothing that I said moved him; he was cold, and his eyes were dead. Thank God for the phone call that saved my life. If it wasn't for that detective, all three of us would be no longer.

Now I had been around my share of street niggas, but none were like Tre. He was unsalvageable, beyond reproach. You were never supposed to let yourself get so savage to the point where you were about to murder the woman you claimed to love so much. Maybe I was naïve, but I knew Rico, Kalief or Quentin would never do no shit like that. It was them damn Carter niggas that seemed to have a little bit too much of the savage gene in their blood.

His father, Tre Carter Sr., was a beast. He didn't let shit slide and was quick to blow a nigga's head clean off. I had heard of him before I even knew Tre. He was the biggest supplier in the Midwest before he got locked up. Niggas spoke highly of him all through the hood. He was loved, respected, and most of all, feared. He passed that on to his punk-ass junior because before Tre even moved here, his name was ringin' bells. That was all Rico talked about was his man's coming to take over the D. I never imagined Tre to be the guy that I fell in love with. We had gotten off to a rocky start. He was nothing like what Isabella had described. She said he was nice and charming and all that shit. She couldn't have been more wrong.

She should have said he was blind and stupid, cuz he surely acted like I was ugly or didn't exist when we first met. I couldn't read him for the life of me and he met my fire with water, not more fire. He straight up put me out. Who knew the initially tumultuous introduction would turn into love? Now look where we were. I should've known better than to get involved in anything Isabella was offering.

After all those nights of our three to four-hour long talks, I should have known it was some underlying bullshit. But the need for money outweighed my better judgment and I joined in on her little plan to break Tre's heart. How I wished I wouldn't have done that. I would've eventually met him anyway and we could've had a real chance. Now all of that was ruined because I can't and won't be with someone who would just end my life without even considering my explanation.

It had hurt so bad to stand there and plead with him not to kill me. I had to explain myself to a man I had been sleeping with for months, someone who I had professed my love to, someone who claimed they loved me too. He reopened wounds I had been trying to heal for months. He traumatized me all over again. He triggered the Post Traumatic Stress Disorder I was finally getting over. He fucked me up so bad that I hadn't even been able to sleep alone. Thank God Isabella and baby Lola were still here to keep me company.

Speaking of Isabella, her and her man were still on bad terms. All they did was argue. Thank God for soundproof walls cuz their poor baby wouldn't be able to stand it. He kept begging her to go back home with him, but she wouldn't budge. That stubborn shit ran in the family. I could tell Isabella was up to something. I felt sorry for Chase because I knew my cousin was a muthafucka. When she wanted revenge, she got it. At this point, even I thought he had had enough, but that wasn't the case. She was plotting something, and I didn't even wanna know what it was.

ISABELLA

I was so in love with my perfect little girl. She had my eyes, nose, and hair and Chase's lips. She was the most precious thing and watching her sleep brought about peace, but it was only momentary. As soon as Chase came near me I was enraged, and that euphoric feeling immediately dissipated. I couldn't stand the sight of him. He literally made me sick.

"Lola sleep? We need to talk," he said, standing there looking stupid as hell.

"Yes, she is but I'm not in the mood to speak to you."

"Well, I am. Just let me say what I need to say then I'll go."

I rolled my eyes and prepared to listen to him go on and on about nothing. This was probably his fifth time trying to have the "Come back to California" conversation with me and I was completely over it.

"Let's go in the other room," I suggested, and he followed me out.

As soon as we got into my bedroom, he started that beggin-ass bullshit.

"Baby, I love you and I'm sorry, okay? I'm sorry for everything I put you through, I'm sorry for chokin' you, I'm sorry that I hurt you. But damn, my ex-wife just got killed. She would have never met that fate if it wasn't for me. I feel like shit. I don't have nobody but you and my baby, and you not even fuckin' wit' me. You don't even understand what I'm goin' through right now. It's either that, or you really don't give a fuck about me."

"Yeah, nice try nigga," I spat and turned my back to him.

One thing he wasn't gonna do was try to reverse psych my ass. I wasn't dumb in the least, so I knew this was just a ploy to get sympathy for me to let up and allow him in my emotional space again. It wasn't happening.

"What?" he asked angrily, turning me back to face him.

I could see his veins bulging. His fist balled against his will and his eyes filled with tears and hatred.

"You heard me. I don't give a fuck about your wife. Fuck her and fuck you too. Go be with that bitch that you had at the hotel."

"Isabella, I swear to God if you keep playin' wit' me, I will leave yo' ass and never come back."

"Bye."

He snatched me by my shirt and pushed me into the wall behind us.

"Please stop. I love you." His nostrils flared as tears poured down his cheeks.

"Fuck you."

"Ughhhhh! Why are you being like this?"

"I don't want to be with you. I want you to be a good father to Lola, and me and you can just be done."

"You don't mean that," he sighed as he let my collar go.

"I do. I just need some space. I need time."

"Isabella, no," he objected, wiping his eyes.

"Please, Chase? I don't wanna be with you right now."

"How are we supposed to be a family for Lola and you tryna leave me? How?"

"We'll figure it out."

At this point, I was done. I was not about to stress myself. I had a child to raise and this arguing shit wasn't helping.

"I swear on everything I love..."

"What? What you gone do, Chase? Kill me? You still threatening me?"

"Nah, I put this on Lola Elise Greene, I am going to fucking kill you." He kissed my forehead then left the room.

I couldn't lie, I was a little scared but I'm Isabella Maria DeMichael, don't shit get to me but empty pockets. If he wanted to act a fool, then it was gon' be two fools.

KIA

"So, when you leavin' this nigga?" Dro asked me as he sparked a blunt.

"Please don't start."

"Fuck you mean, don't start? You think I'm about to keep sneakin' around with *my* fuckin' woman? Who the fuck you think I am, some type of hoe-nigga or somethin'?"

"No, but you know the situation. I can't just leave," I tried to explain, but he wasn't tryna hear that shit.

"Yeah, you can. You a grown-ass woman, Kia. You don't gotta be with nobody you don't wanna be with, except me. You mine. That's *my* pussy."

"Damien..."

"Kia," he said, mocking me.

"Can we just enjoy the moment and stop talkin' about Rico?"

"Fuck no. You either leave that nigga or he leavin' this earth in a shallow grave."

I knew he was serious as all hell. I didn't want Rico to die behind my selfishness.

"You don't have to do any of that if you give me time."

"It takes literally a thirty-second phone call to tell that nigga y'all done. This my last time telling you this," he warned, taking a long pull from his blunt.

"Stop with the threats, baby. You do anything to Rico and we not gon' be together either."

"You defending this nigga now?"

"No, but you better not touch him."

"Fuck, you Kia," he spat and got up from where we were sitting in his living room.

"Nah, fuck you. Niggas can never be understanding. You're not in my situation. When you so-called had to cut off your bitch, you needed time," I reminded him.

"No, I didn't. I sent that bitch on her way and came back to get you. Now look at yo' dumb ass. Can't show me the same courtesy cuz you still in love wit' that nigga."

"Okay, Dro," I countered.

"A'ight, bitch," he spat and walked away.

I just sat there, unbothered. He was not about to get to me. If I said I needed time, then I needed time. I didn't want any drama from Rico, so I had to move the right way. If he couldn't understand that then fuck him.

I got up to go pack some of my things. I was leaving to clear my head. I walked into our bedroom and there he was, lying in bed, chewing on a toothpick. His eyes cut into me and gave me the dirtiest, most hateful look. I shook it off, grabbed my overnight bag, and packed some clothes.

"Going to lay up wit' that nigga, huh," he chuckled as he spoke.

"Actually no. Just need to get away from you before something bad happens."

"Yeah a'ight, Kia. Have fun suckin' his dick."

"Stop talkin' to me, hoe," I snapped, finally.

"What the fuck you just call me?" He rose up and got out of bed, approaching me.

I knew I had said the wrong thing. He towered over me, scowling like a junkyard pitbull.

"You just called me a bit—" I couldn't even finish before he had my neck in his hand.

"Watch yo' fuckin mouth, bitch!" he yelled with rage in his eyes.

"Fuck you, hoe-ass nigga!"

Oddly, he let me go and I continued to pack. Once I had all my things, I exited the closet and Dro was standing against the door to our bedroom, taunting me.

"Excuse me," I said, waiting for him to move.

"You not goin' nowhere."

"Watch out, Dro."

"Call me Dro again!"

"*Dro,* move out my way."

He smacked the bag from my hand. Then he picked it up and started emptying the contents onto the floor. He threw the bag clean across the room.

"I fuckin' said you aint goin' nowhere." He was too calm for my liking.

That always meant that he was about to pop off sooner than later. Anxiety washed over me as I prepared myself for what he was about to do next. I wanted to bolt out the room and just leave but I was thrown off. I didn't know which way to go. Then I caught that glare in his eyes that let me know he was up to no good.

"Don't start," I warned, inching back until I was against the closet door.

"Or what's gon' happen?"

"Boy get out my face," I rolled my eyes as he continued to walk toward me.

"Take yo' pants off Kia, I'm tryna see somethin'."

"Bye, Dro!"

"Man come here!" He grabbed me and choked me until I got wet as hell.

"Babyyy," I cooed.

"I forgot you like that shit. Now take them raggedy-ass leggings off and lemme eat that pussy."

I did as I was told. So, as you can see, nothing has changed. I still couldn't leave Dro and I wasn't quite through with Rico yet either. The thrill of it all had me in deep. Did I love both of them? Hell yes. If I could just have them both forever I would, but I know that wouldn't happen even in my wildest dreams.

MARCUS

"Pops, chill a'ight? It ain't even that deep," I tried to reason with my dad, but he was not listening.

I was happy as hell he was out of prison, but he could spare me the sermon about Tre.

"Boy, I oughta kill yo' simple ass! What in the hell would possess you to set your own damn brother up for murder? All these years you been in the murder game and yo' ass don't know shit about forensics and time of death? You don't know shit about autopsy reports?" He yelled at me like I was a fuckin' child.

"Yeah, I do. I was just tryna teach him a lesson."

"Teach him a lesson about what? Some shit that happened a long time ago? You not even with that bitch, why do you care if she let the next nigga have some of that pussy? The pussy wasn't yours. It's never yours, it's just your turn, son."

"Well, it was my turn and that nigga cut in and took my shit. I had to get DNA tests done on my kids. Do you know how that feels?"

"Yes! I got goddamn DNA tests done on y'all peanut head-ass negroes. Worst day of my life when it came back that y'all were mine." He burst out laughing and I couldn't help but laugh too.

"Dad, I know you don't like what I did, but at least I didn't kill him."

"Boy, if you even think about killing my first born," he warned.

"Chill pops, as much as I hate that nigga, I wouldn't dare."

"I'd put a bullet right between yo' beady little eyes. I want you to lay low, don't go near that damn warehouse and wait for this shit to die down. You need to have somebody torch that fuckin' place. It's a cesspool of evidence and murder convictions. You've come a long way, son, but you still got a long way to go if you wanna be a real killer. That place should have been gone the minute they figured she had been killed at a warehouse. Don't let anger and revenge get you locked up. As a matter-of-fact, give me keys to all your warehouses. I need to do an inspection anyway. Make sure you still know what you're doing."

I surrendered the keys after realizing everything he said was true. I had let anger blind me and have me out here messy as hell. I had severely fallen off my game. All my brother had to do was point them bastards in my direction and I was as good as gone. I'd have so many consecutive life sentences. He had so much dirt and evidence on me, I may as well commit suicide, cuz I'd never see the light of day again.

"I'm gon' let you do what do, but just know, I got this."

"Yeah, I thought you did, but you seem like you tryna go to prison. But on another note, you talked to your brother, Devin, or Chase or whatever he's calling himself these days?"

"Of course. We move weight together, so I gotta stay up wit' him. I just hate that bitch he with. You know, she's the reason all this shit happened in the first place. If it wasn't for her, me and Scoot would have never had beef."

"*Nobody* should have been the reason, jackass. You never cease to amaze me with your pettiness. You get that feminine shit from yo' mama. Y'all are exactly alike, bitter, scorned and plain ruthless. Only difference is, you stupid." My dad stayed crackin' on me.

"Don't bring my mama into this," I warned.

"Or what? Nigga, I made you, you think you scare me? You just like that ole shady bitch. You know she tried to kill me one time? Boy, yo' mama was a bad muhfucka."

"I'm sure she had her reasons."

"She thought I was cheating with the neighbor. The neighbor was damn near old enough to be my grandmother!"

We both burst out laughing,

"Damn, I guess she was a little crazy huh?"

"And all that venom and rage went right into you, my little demon seed. I always knew you would be the one." He patted my shoulder and put on his leather hat with that signature red feather and got up to leave.

"I ain't that bad."

"You much worse, son. I expect you to make this shit right. Y'all boys are my pride and joy and if anything happens to either one of you, yo' old man won't have nothin' to live for. I hustled for y'all. I created avenues for y'all to have whatever you needed and wanted, and this is not how I planned for you to turn out. I barely even raised Chase, but he seems to be the only one with some sense."

"Don't say that."

"Yeah whatever, boy. Make it right, Marcus, or I'll make it right for you. Don't think cuz I been in prison that anything has changed. I still got the same connects, plus more. I'll put your ass out of commission," he threatened.

I didn't doubt my father one bit. Whatever he wanted to happen, it happened. He was still as powerful as the day he got locked up. He was supposed to serve twenty years but only did four. So, I had no feelings of uncertainty when he said he would do something. I didn't wanna go toe-to-toe with the big dogs. Especially not Tre Sr. He was a walking death sentence. However, even after the threats and pep talk, I still had plans for my brother. God wasn't done with him, and neither was I.

2

CHAOS AND CALAMITY

RICO

Kia was still playing games. She was stupid if she thought I didn't know about her and Dro sneakin' around. The worst part of it all was that Jas knew and had straight up lied to my face for her two-timin' ass friend. That brother-sister shit was dead. That was my last time feeling betrayed by her. I couldn't believe these last three years of friendship meant nothing to her. How was she more loyal to a bitch than her "brother?"

Luckily, all my time was being spent trying to get Tre out of prison. I couldn't really focus on her because I was always handling some business of his, meeting with his lawyers and making sure he was good. If Kia was in my face at this moment, I would probably kill her, so good thing she was ghost. Words couldn't even convey how done I was with her. I was just as done with her as I was Jasmine. Those two bitches could die together for all I cared.

"You need anything else?" the bartender, Alesia asked me as I found myself in the same strip club that led me to Kia's sister.

"Nah, I'm good." I waved her off after she served me my Hennessy.

I was there for Mercedes and nothing more. When I saw that beautiful body grace the stage, my dick instantly grew hard. She was still gorgeous as ever and it had been a long six months since I'd seen her. I knew she probably hated my guts, but I wanted to be in hers, so I made my way to the stage and started making it rain hundreds. All the other dancers looked on with amazement and jealousy plastered over their made-up faces. I saw the shock on Mercedes' face when she realized those bills weren't ones.

She danced even harder as I continued to make the bills fall all over the stage. She didn't know who was throwing the money, but I bet if she knew it was me, she would have stopped. I waited for her to finish then I approached her when she climbed off stage.

"Rico, what are you doing here?" She cut her eyes at me.

"I came to see you, love."

"I know that wasn't you throwing all those hundreds."

"Chill, you know I'm the only nigga in here wit' that kinda cash. Don't act brand new baby."

"What do you want?" She frowned with her arms folded.

"I wanted to check on you, see how you were doing. You still lookin' good as the day you blocked me." I grinned, hoping to break the ice that she had in her glare.

"I'm fine, but I was doing better before I saw you."

"You ain't gotta be like that Cedes." I poked out my lip, hoping she would fall for my bullshit.

"What do you want, Rico?"

"You."

"You had me and acted like a damn fool. You ruined that."

"I treated you like a fuckin' princess, Mercedes," I reminded her.

"Yeah and you think I don't know about you and my sister? You think we hadn't talked?"

"Oh yeah? Did she tell you how I bought her a ring that cost well over a quarter of a million dollars and she somewhere fuckin' my enemy right now? Did she tell you how I got my shit together for her and guess what, Mercedes, she out here in a three-hundred-thou-sand-dollar ring of mine getting fucked by my *rival*. I don't wanna hear shit about yo' bitch-ass sister right now."

"Don't talk about her like that."

"Man, fuck her. When I met you, I had no idea that y'all were related. She clearly doesn't want to be with me."

"So, now you back in my face cuz she played you. Bye, Rico, have a nice night," she said and walked off.

She was switching that fat ass so hard I was stuck for a second. I knew I had blown it with her, but it was worth a try. I guess it was back to the drawing board for me. I had a lot to think about and I had a ring to get back from a two-timing, snake-ass hoe.

JASMINE

Between Tre and his jail calls and Rico calling, texting, and cursing me out, I couldn't get any sleep. I decided to just answer the phone for Rico since he wasn't gonna stop ringing my shit.

"What?" I hissed with much attitude.

"What? I know you saw me calling you."

"So? I also saw all the expletives you used in those text messages as well. It's 9 o'clock in the morning and you think I'm about to be arguing with yo' mad ass at this time of day? I think the fuck not."

"So, what's good? Why you been lyin' to me so much? I thought we were better than that, Jas."

"We not. Kia is my best friend. My loyalty lies with her and you should know that. The same way your loyalty lies with Tre. You wanted to give him my number and address, so he could constantly call and write me," I reminded him.

"That nigga love you! I'm not about to deny him some shit he had before he went to prison. Was he not beatin' that pussy down before he was arrested? *Wrongfully*, might I add."

"It doesn't matter. He put a gun in my mouth, Rico."

There was an awkward pause on his end. I knew that information was new to him. Tre certainly wasn't going to tell him that.

"Damn, I ain't know that."

"Well now you do. How do you think I felt? After what happened to me, you think I wanna fuck with a man that would traumatize me all over again? He really thought I would set him up after all that we had been through."

"Jas, I'm sorry."

"No, you good. Just leave me alone okay, Rico."

"Nah, I'm outside, open the door."

Reluctantly, I got up from my cozy bed and threw on my house-coat and slippers to let him in.

"Why are you here?" I asked, wiping my eyes.

"You ugly as hell in the morning. I don't see why my nigga wanna be with you so bad," he chuckled as he stepped inside.

"It ain't for you to worry about."

"Anywho, I need a favor and if you tell me no, I'm gonna have to shoot your best friend."

"I know you didn't bring yo' raggedy ass over my house to threaten me."

"I did, now I need you to get that bitch over here, so I can get my ring. That's the least you could do since you've been covering for her lyin' ass this whole time."

"What makes you think I'm involved in anything?"

"Jas, I'm not in the mood. You just admitted you knew, stop playin' wit' me before I hurt you," he warned.

When Rico talked calm, I knew he was serious.

"Don't threaten me. You know that never ends well."

"Just get the bitch over here! Call her now and tell her to come over. I just want my ring and nothin' else. I'm not gon' say the shit again."

"Get the fuck out!" I yelled at him.

He snatched me by my neck so fast and threw me onto the couch behind us. He had gotten on top of me and started choking the fuck out of me. He looked completely out of his mind and for the first time, I was honestly scared.

"Call that bitch right now!"

When he let me go, I reared my hand back so far and slapped him as hard as I could. Then, I started swinging.

"Bitch, don't you ever!" I screamed as I continued raining blows to his face.

He wasn't ready. I had hit him about four times before he even realized it.

"Jas, a'ight stop!" He tried to shield his face from the attack, but I had gotten that nose and bottom lip and they both were leaking.

"Get yo' crazy ass off me, bitch," I tried to push him off, but he was too heavy.

"Just call her, please, Jas. You know she doin' me dirty as fuck right now."

"No! Now get the fuck off me."

Then he pulled out a gun. If I didn't think our friendship was over before, it was now. Did I not just say what Tre did? Did I not tell him about the trauma I had been dealing with?

"Really, Rico?" I asked as he cocked it with his eyes narrowed on me.

"Fuckin' really, bitch. Now call her and she better come or I'm putting a bullet in you," he seethed through gritted teeth.

I pulled out my phone and dialed her. I didn't even care anymore. After this, I was done with Rico forever.

"Hey, Kia."

"Hey, boo, you sound weird. What's wrong?"

Rico pressed the gun against my cheek, letting me know not to try no funny shit.

"Girl just stressing. I really need a friend right now."

"You at home? I'll come over."

"Yeah and bring food."

"All right, I'm on my way," she said and hung up.

Rico had returned to human form from his demonic outburst. That psychotic look he had was gone. It didn't matter from this point on. I didn't know a Rico.

"That's all you had to do. You always wanna be difficult," he added, trying to lighten the mood.

I was still outdone that he had put his hands on me. But that bloody lip and nose I gave him made me feel better. At least Kia would know that I was forced and tried to fight.

I stayed completely silent until she got here. I had nothing to say, but Rico kept trying to talk to me. I wanted to slit his fuckin' throat, but the gun he had stopped me from trying anything stupid.

When the doorbell rang, I prepared myself for what was about to happen next. My fears immediately went from a ten to a hundred when I opened the door and Kia stood there smiling accompanied by Dro. I froze in my tracks momentarily until Rico snatched the door open and started going crazy.

"Bitch, I should kill you," was all I heard before Dro and him started fighting.

Thank God, he was there to disarm Rico and stop him from doing something we all would regret. That blow that knocked Rico off his feet had managed to also knock the gun from his hand. I grabbed it and held onto it while the two men battled to the death right in front of us. Kia was visibly upset and had started crying. She just stared at me like I was crazy. We both tried to break up the fight, but they wouldn't stop coming for each other. They both had the hands and I was scared to keep getting in the middle because if I got hit, I was shooting somebody.

"Oh my God, please stop!" I yelled as I pointed the gun at both of them.

"Jas put that damn gun down," Rico yelled at me, but I wasn't listening.

I wanted them to stop destroying my house. I saw Kia reach for something in her purse. It was a taser and she used it to shock both of their crazy asses. They both fell to the floor, shaking like they were having a seizure.

"This is what the fuck you called me over here for?" She looked at me with tears in her eyes.

"Kia, what? No! This nigga made—"

"Bitch, fuck you," she screamed.

"Gimme my fuckin' ring bitch!" Rico managed to say as he pulled himself from the floor.

She reluctantly took it off and let it drop from her hand to the floor.

"Neither of you better ever speak to me again," she spat then bolted out of the door.

I couldn't believe her. She knew damn well I would never betray her, but she was really standing here trying to end our friendship when she knew Rico had a way of getting what he wanted. I just let her leave. I was too exhausted to chase after her. I would see her when she calmed down.

"Get the fuck out of my house before I kill you," I told Rico.

He did as he was told. Once Dro regained his composure, he looked at me to apologize.

"I will pay for everything. I'm so sorry about this sweetheart," he told me as he dusted himself off.

"It's fine, Dro, you were only trying to protect yourself," I assured him as I looked around at all the damage that was done to my new townhouse.

"Nah, I got this. I promise, a'ight? That shit was out of hand, but I wasn't about to let that crazy nigga hurt neither one of y'all."

"Thank you."

He then adjusted his clothing and turned to leave.

"Did she get in the car with Rico?" Dro asked after stepping back into my house.

"No, she didn't drive?"

"Nah, she rode with me and she's not in my car."

We both tried calling her phone, but it was going to voicemail.

"Mannnn, you know that girl is crazy," he sighed looking to me to tell him where she was.

"She'll probably just go home."

"I hope so. If it's not too much trouble, can I get your number just in case I can't find her?"

"Sure." I input my number in his phone and saved it.

"Thanks, and sorry again. How much them lamps run you for?"

"Honestly?" I knew Dro had money, so I don't know why I was being modest. "A thousand dollars."

"Goddamn, for some lamps? What were they made out of, Beyonce's tears?"

"No, you didn't," I cackled. "They were hand-blown tempered glass. That shit costs."

"Well, this should cover it," he handed me a wad of money and then dipped.

I was left to clean up the mess that was now my living room. I was just happy that Isabella and Lola had left for the day. I wouldn't have wanted my baby cousin here during all this turmoil.

KIA

It was freezing outside, and my dumb ass decided to walk off like I was dressed for this frigid-ass weather. I was shivering like a fiend in a crack house. I trudged up the pavement through Jas's complex and made my way to the exit. I was so mad right now, I didn't even care. I just had to get out of that situation before I snapped. I couldn't believe Jas, my best friend, had set me up. Like why the fuck would she do that?

I couldn't even think of an answer. I was completely out of my mind. I wandered aimlessly for a while, searching through my phone when I realized I'd deleted the Uber app. I found the nearest coffee shop and stepped inside to shield myself from the cold. My Northface hoodie was trash at keeping me warm, not to mention this thin-ass pair of leggings. When I got in, I ordered a coffee and sat down. I made a mental note to look up some houses when I got home because I was moving, and no one would know where it would be.

I had several missed calls, but I wasn't in the mood to talk to anyone. I was fiery mad and embarrassed. My dreams had been shattered right in my face. Dro was probably happy as hell, but I wasn't. I loved Rico. I really did. I loved his face, his smile. I loved those wicked eyes of his. I loved how he looked when he was angry. I loved how he looked when he was sad. He was the cutest when he was happy. But he looked the best when we made love. All those emotions surfaced, and I got to see every expression he owned.

His eyes held a powerful glance that made me shudder with excitement and lust. You ever just stared at yo' nigga and got turned on? That's how it was with Rico. I wasn't ready to stop seeing his face yet, and that was what made it so hard for me to let go. I remember the first time we met. It was the craziest introduction, but we ended up together.

Jas and I were out celebrating our two-year friendship anniversary. We were at this poolhall/bar in downtown Detroit. It was a mixed crowd, so the atmosphere was lit. Everybody was drinking and having fun. The white girls in there had us super turnt, and we were drunk and disorderly as fuck.

Jas was lookin' fuckable in her two-piece leopard print skirt. Her hair was silky, jet-black and hung to the middle of her back. I wasn't surprised when some fine-ass dude came up to her. By the way they exchanged greetings, I could tell they knew each other. Then another dude breezed past me and almost knocked me down trying to fight some drunk guy that probably just stepped on his shoe. He crushed my foot in the process. I winced in pain as he stopped to whisper an apology before he got to dude and started swinging. A huge brawl broke out behind us and the guy that was talking to Jas had rushed to jump into the fight. I was trying to get the hell out, but that dude had damn-near injured my foot.

Those guys were knocking everything over, but at least they were fist fighting, I thought to myself. Before I could even process that thought, I heard gunshots ring out. We all ducked as the security guards scrambled to secure the premises. Everyone started running in every direction and I was surprised when Jas' friend came back and grabbed us, followed by the guy who stepped on my foot that was now in serious pain. I limped toward the exit, and the guys pushed through the crowd, ushering us out and to our car.

"Y'all good," the brown skinned one asked us.

"Yes, Kalief, we are fine. Thank you," she responded but I had a nasty look on my face.

I wasn't okay at all. My foot was aching like hell as I stood there shooting daggers at the guy who had hurt me.

"Sorry again for your foot, Kia," the light skinned guy said to me.

"How'd you know my name?"

He pointed at Jas who gave me a smirk. I hope he wasn't trying to talk to me cuz I wasn't in any sort of mood. My shit was throbbing, and I really wanted to get in the passenger seat and go home. I simply nodded and rolled my eyes.

"It's a problem, Miss Kia," he eyed me.

"Kia, this is Rico, my homeboy." Jas smiled trying to ease the tension.

"Okay," was all I had to say.

"What's her problem," Rico asked Jas.

"My problem is you stepping on my damn foot to go fight some stupid-ass niggas in a bar."

"And I apologized. What you want, a lawsuit," he spat.

"No, I want y'all stupid niggas to stop disrupting other people's fun cuz y'all too macho to have a good time at a bar."

"Sweetheart, you have no idea what you talkin' about or who you talkin' to."

"Excuse me?"

"You must never heard of me before."

"You must have never heard that bars are for fun and drinks, not fighting and stepping on women's feet," I shot back.

"I fuckin' said sorry!" His face was stern, and his body language was aggressive.

"Sorry ain't gon' help my foot, nigga," I yelled back.

"Yo, Jas what the fuck wrong wit' yo' girl, dog?"

"Nah, what the fuck wrong wit' you yellin' at her like you ain't got no sense?" Jas jumped in, and I was glad she had my back.

"I forgot you one of them," Rico chuckled and turned his attention back toward me.

"Okay, you hurt my friend's foot, don't expect her to be nice to you."

"You want me to rub yo' feet," he smiled at me. His smile was nothing short of infectious.

"Hell no. I want you to get the fuck out my face."

"Ayo, chill. I'm offering to help yo' lil ugly ass feel better but if you gon' act stank then fuck you and yo' foot. I hope that bitch broke," he spat.

Why he went that far, I didn't know, but I did see Jas rushing toward him. She pushed him into my car and was all up in his face yelling for him not to disrespect me again. For some reason, he listened to her.

"Stupid-ass bitch," I mumbled folding my arms.

"Hol' up, what the fuck you just call me?" he gave me a dirty look.

"You heard me."

"Listen, just cuz you pretty don't mean I won't choke yo' ass out."

"Try it," I heard Jas say.

"Mind yo' business, light skin," Rico said pointing to her.

"Get 'em, Jas," I instigated from the sidelines.

"Now I was gone offer to rub yo' crusty-ass feet but you just fucked that up."

"That's fine," I remarked with folded arms.

If this rude-ass nigga thought he was about to get next to me by offering me a foot rub, he was right. Rico was sexy as fuck and had that look in his eyes. I just knew he would do some ungodly things to me.

"Well let me follow y'all home, you know, to make sure you get in safe," he suggested.

"You do that," Jas answered before I could.

When I saw the car that he was driving my eyes saw dollar signs like the gold-diggin' hoodrat I always knew I was.

"Girl, who is he," I asked Jas.

"My friend. He like you though," she grinned.

"Well shit, I like him too."

"Yassss, I knew you would. He's your type."

"And what's my type?"

"Flashy, disrespectful and gangsta."

"You know me well, bestie," we both giggled.

Once we got home, we all started playing cards and talking. Rico was talking about some trip he had to California in a few days. He most likely had a bitch there since he said it was his third time this month. I wasn't stupid, I knew what was up.

After that night ended with Rico rubbing my foot and getting himself worked up trying to fuck me and being unsuccessful, he went on his trip and came back in hot pursuit. He was all over me the minute he got back to Detroit. He took me out, courted me, and acted like a whole gentleman. I was surprised to say the least. Now look at us. Fighting and arguing like we never even made love before.

I was still very much confused about where I wanted to be, but I did know that I wasn't done with either of them. It was all Rico's fault that I had fallen into the arms of another man. If he wouldn't have been accusing me of cheating and he hadn't been fucking around with my sister, then we'd probably be married with a baby on the way. But no, he had to go and be a typical nigga.

The bell to the Biggby coffee shop chimed causing me to look up. In walked Rico, scowling like a dog and looking around for me. I looked down and pretended not to see him.

"You a piece of shit, you know that?" he said as he approached the table.

"I thought we were done. Why are you following me around if you done?"

"Don't fuckin' worry about it," he said, taking a seat at my table.

He just stared at me, angrily, burning a hole into my skin with his fiery eyes.

"So, you came here to look at me?"

"Tryna figure out what I saw in you."

"That's real cute. But it's probably the same thing I saw in you, nothing."

"The same shit that had you losin' yo' damn mind every time I stuck my dick in you, though," he chuckled.

"And the same shit that had you losin' yours when I sucked the soul outta you."

"That's cool. If it wasn't so many witnesses I'd blow yo' fuckin' brains out," he threatened while grabbing on his gun.

Without hesitation, I grabbed and kissed him. He didn't fight, just palmed the back of my head. When we broke from the kiss, all he said was, "Let's go," and I followed him to his car.

Once inside, he drove to his house and the cycle began again. We were making hot love in his bed all night. It was so emotionally intense. He had never shown me that side of him before. The nigga was damn near crying and telling me he loved me.

"You gon' stay? Huh? Where you goin', Ki?" Rico asked as he feverishly pounded me into submission.

"Ricoooo, pleaseeee!" I shouted as he brought me to orgasm for the second time.

"Nah, you gon' stop disrespectin' me, Kia. I know I hurt you, but okay, I'm done, I swear," he sounded like he was on the verge of tears.

The emotion in his voice made me pity him. I was destroying him. I had destroyed him.

"You fuckin' disrespected me!" I shouted back as he went deeper inside me.

"I know! I fuckin' know baby and I'm sorry." Tears filled his red eyes and slid down his cheeks.

I was scared at this point. When a nigga cry over you, he's too far gone.

"Baby don't cry, please," I comforted him, wiping the tears from his face.

"You see how you got me? You see how fuckin' weak you got me?!"

He then flipped me onto my stomach and slipped his hand around my throat. His pounding was so brutal I couldn't even recall how many times I came or squirted. All I knew was that we had to sleep in another room because not only were the sheets wet, so was the mattress.

Rico held me so tight while we slept. This was the Rico I wanted. He used to make me so happy, then when it all started going bad, he lost me. Now, he was trying to get back to my heart. I didn't know what would happen in the future but for now, this was where I wanted to be. When I woke up the next morning and my ring was back on my finger, it was solidified.

3

SOMETHING UP MY SLEEVE
ISABELLA

I was on a flight to Florida to see my mother. I was going to try and convince her to move to Detroit for a while, so she could meet Lola and watch her while I worked. By work, I meant work Chase's nerves. I really don't know why I wanted to hurt him so bad, but I did, and I was. Oh, I remember, because he almost killed me. He had no idea how painful that experience was for me. At that point, I thought that nigga loved me more than anything.

I thought Chase was my fuckin' rider. He had my back through it all and stayed with me despite the situation with his brothers. I don't know too many men that would do that, but Chase and I seemed to have a special type of bond. One that nobody could break. But one simple sentence caused him to say, "Fuck that bond" and wrap his filthy hands so tight around my neck that I lost consciousness and almost lost our baby. I was still very much hurt about that. Even though she and I survived, the thought of him forgetting who I was and what I meant to him made me deeply resent him.

When I wanted revenge, I got it. You should know that by now. I was about to completely and utterly obliterate Chase's heart and emotions. He would never love a bitch again, and if he did, it would never be the same. Hopefully, I could convince my mom to come back with me, so my plan could take motion.

All during the plane ride, I rehearsed my speech to my mom and prayed that she would be willing to come back with me, at least for a few months. When we landed I got in the cab and headed straight to my late father's estate. I didn't bring luggage cuz I wasn't staying. I was getting her, and we were hopping on the plane back to Detroit, hopefully.

The driver dropped me off. I gave him a hefty tip and skipped up to the large pinewood doors that guarded the mansion. I rang the doorbell and seconds later, there was my mother, smiling ear-to-ear.

"Bella?!" she gasped, pulling me into a hug.

"Mom, how I've missed you!" I hugged her even tighter.

"Come in." She ushered me inside and into the huge living room that could've been another house.

"So, how are you enjoying it here?" I asked her, hiding my true intentions.

"I love it. This house is huge. I still haven't seen all of it."

"Well, Mom, you know I just had a baby, right?"

"What? Where is she? Is it a boy or a girl? By who?" She asked a million questions before I could even get one answer out.

"She's in Michigan with my cousin, Jasmine. Her name is Lola and her dad is Chase. My boyfriend. She's two months."

"Oh, my goodness, my baby don' had a baby," she cheered.

"Yes, and I would like for you to meet her."

"I would love to. I know she can't ride a plane here, so I guess I'll have to come back to Michigan with you," she suggested, and I couldn't have been happier.

My plan was going off without a hitch.

"Yes, Mom, so I have a plane ticket for you to come with me. Now, though."

"Well, let me pack some essentials and I guess I can get anything else I need when I get there, huh?"

"Yes, I have you a nice place to stay. It's a lot smaller than this but it's nice."

"Baby, I don't need all this room. I told you it's parts of this house I haven't even been in yet." She chuckled then went to pack.

"How long can you stay?"

"As long as you need. I wanna get to know my grandbaby. I want to see her grow up. I'll leave when it's time, sugar," she said and continued up the grand staircase to her room.

Yesssss! I couldn't believe how easy it was to get her to come back with me. I guess it was meant to be. Chase was in for a rude awakening when I got back. It was no more living at Jas' house. He wasn't even gonna know where I live. I had found a nice house in a small city called Franklin Hills. I knew my mom would love it because it looked like time stood still there. It was outdated and country, but the homes were elegant and expensive.

Once my mother packed, we headed back out and to the airport. We boarded the plane and were on our way back to Michigan, just that fast. I was used to getting my way but geez, there was no delay on the gratification this time. I knew my mom felt guilty about missing out on me growing up so that was part of the reason, but she also seemed genuinely happy to have a granddaughter.

Once the plane landed, we hailed a cab back to the new house I had set up for her. I was having Jas bring Lola over and she was set to arrive any minute. I helped my mom unpack and get comfortable while I got dinner started. I was so glad I thought ahead and had the house furnished and baby-proofed to make the stay here perfect. Everything looked great and now all I had to do was wait for my beauty to get here. When the doorbell rang, it was Jas bringing in my sugarplum with all her things.

"Hey, boo, thanks for watching her for me," I said as I kissed Jas on the cheek.

"Anytime, cuz. Auntie Karen?" Jas gasped as she realized who was sitting on the couch.

I had shown her pictures of my mom because I knew she may not recognize her after so many years.

"Jasmine?! My you have grown up to be absolutely gorgeous. You and Izzy are both so stunning!"

"Thank you! How have you been?" She took a seat next to my mom.

"Better. I've been amazing since I kicked my habit, but enough about me, let me see this bundle of joy."

Jas lifted the blanket and there was my precious baby, looking up at them and smiling like the perfect angel she was.

"Oh myyyy, isn't she the most beautiful little thing. Little Lola, hi," she squealed, and my baby must have loved it because she was laughing and kicking her feet.

"Let me wash my hands so I can hold her." My mom got up to go to the bathroom.

She came back, unstrapped Lola from her car seat and cradled her, rocking her gently while they both stared lovingly into each other's eyes. Fuck the Chase shit, I was genuinely happy that my mom was here spending time with her granddaughter. It warmed my heart to see how nurturing she could be without the influence of drugs. I wished I could have experienced more of that, but the past was the past and everyone had a vice. I had forgiven her long ago. Now, I just wanted her here so she wouldn't miss more time with her family.

"I'm so glad you decided to come to Florida. I wouldn't miss this for the world. She is so precious, just like you Izzy," my mom said to me.

"I know, and I wouldn't have you miss it. I'm so happy I have my family. Y'all have been so helpful to me. Like Jas, I really don't know what I would have done without you. Ma, you know she helped me get ready to go to the hospital when my water broke, and she stayed there until I delivered."

"I'm glad you girls are keeping the meaning of family alive."

"We are, Auntie Karen. I'm just so glad you came here! It is really good seeing you." She hugged and kissed my mom on the cheek.

Moments like this were so important. I had the three people that I loved the most, all in my living room. The warmth was intoxicating, something I could get used to. All those years, I didn't have or see this part of my family. I saw my dad, but rarely, and it was never anything memorable. Then these past couple of years were complete hell.

I can't say there were no enjoyable moments at all, but they were few and far between. All that hot, but meaningless sex leading to inescapable drama that almost cost me my life was something to remember, though. It gave me a rush like no other to hold that much power in my hands over others and survive it all. Dealing with men who were completely psychotic and those with ulterior motives took a toll on me and in turn, I took a toll on them. Nobody was gonna see me lose and in the end, I didn't. I walked away with everything and it honestly made me happy.

I couldn't sit and regret any of the decisions I made because they all worked together for my good. Some people thought money didn't bring happiness, but honestly walking out of there with twenty-five million dollars and knowing I could take care of my mother, sparked a joy inside me that couldn't be diminished. Being able to rub that shit in the faces of those that tried to hurt me made it that much better.

I know they felt like complete fucking losers when it all went down. Especially Tre with his shady ass. I was so happy that he got his ass locked up, twice now. That nigga was still tryna get at me when I came here with Chase the last time. It was so utterly disrespectful, but as much as I hate him, I can't lie and say I never had feelings for him. I also didn't feel like he had ill-intentions, but the way he handled that situation was wrong. Now, he was in love with my cousin. And I honestly wasn't mad at it. If I knew anything about Jas, I knew Tre was her type.

She had been acting terrible toward him and not answering his calls or letters. I guess my plan to break his heart was working after all and she didn't even realize it. She could act tough all she wanted. I knew she missed him. Her whole energy had been off since he got locked up. I knew she was mad at him but that didn't mean her ass wasn't hurt. He fucked up the day he decided to pull a gun on her; I knew that shit had traumatized her in more ways than one.

To have been in a situation where someone you loved tried to kill you then to have the man you actually love to do it again, it was painful to even think about. I knew Chase was still upset about it too, but he had to put that shit aside to get his brother free. I wanted to be there for the reunion when he did get out. I knew Chase had some choice words for his brother.

I had been eavesdropping before I left Chase and I heard that Tre would be getting out soon. No official date, but soon and they were throwing him a welcome home party. I was gonna be there with bells on and Jas didn't know it, but she would be there too. I had a heart to break and I was doing everything in my power to get the job done. Chase had hurt me so damned bad.

Like, have you ever been almost choked to death? Not that cutesy shit where a nigga chokes you and you get all wet and y'all fuck afterwards. No, you're literally staring death in the face and it's the man you love, taking the life away from you. Jas had this happen to her twice, so I knew she would understand why I was on the revenge tip. But I knew she wouldn't wanna be anywhere near Tre, so that was why I wasn't telling her. We were just gonna show up.

UNTITLED

\

RICO

Yeah, I got my bitch back, but I felt bad as hell for her thinking that Jas had set her up. They were best friends and I know she knew Jas was loyal to her. But to tell her the truth would be me admitting to threatening her and putting my hands on her and I just couldn't do that. Kia most definitely wouldn't want shit to do with me then. I had to think of a way to ensure that Kia stayed with me even if she found out.

"Baby, get up and get dressed, we gonna miss our plane," I told Kia who was still asleep from last night.

It was well into midmorning and I had something I wanted to do.

"What plane, Rico?" She was groggy and irritated, but she was still gonna get her ass up.

"The plane I fuckin' bought tickets for, now get the fuck up before you ruin my day," I urged.

She unhappily climbed out of bed looking ugly as hell and went to shower and brush her teeth. She emerged thirty minutes later still unhappy and still frowning.

"You betta put a smile on yo' face, wit' yo' ugly ass," I teased.

She hated being woken up from her sleep.

"Fuck off," she stuck up her middle finger and sat down on the edge of the bed.

"Pack nigga, we gon' be gone for three days. It's gonna be hot so pack swimwear and damn near anything you got cuz all you wear is summer clothes in the winter anyway."

"Heauxs don't get cold." She shrugged before walking into her closet.

"Just hurry up, damn."

Ten minutes later, she had her a couple bags packed. I grabbed them, and she followed me down the steps and out of the front door to the car I had dropping us off at the airport. Once we arrived, we headed to bag check and to sit down for the short wait we had to board the plane. She was still sleepy, so she had little to nothing to say to me. I liked it that way, no questions, no lies.

We boarded the plane and got comfy in our first-class seats. Kia was sleep in no time. It felt like this was confirmation that this was supposed to happen. Nothing had ever gone this easy before. The four-hour and forty-minute flight was quiet. I held my baby close to me and stroked her hair as she slept. I know I didn't show it, but this girl meant the world to me. Nobody, not even me or Kia understood how much I loved her. I didn't know why I felt like this about her, but I did, and nobody was gonna come in the way of what I had.

Once the flight landed, I woke her up and we were on our way to the surprise I had for her. Everything was already planned out. I just needed her to be down for it. As you've probably guessed by now, we were eloping.

"Baby, I know this isn't what you wanted, but I promise we are gonna have a real wedding and a big one. I just need you to be my wife *now*. I can't lose you," I professed to her in our hotel room.

"Aww babe," she shrieked, stroking my face then kissing me.

"So, you'll do it?"

"Yes!"

I was overjoyed. I couldn't believe she would agree to this. This meant she really loved me. She was willing to temporarily abandon her dream for me. I guess she knew I would give her whatever she wanted, and I would. I wanted her to plan the biggest wedding she could think of. I was just glad to have my baby back.

We went to the chapel and as the proceedings went on, there was this satisfied smile on her face. It made me even happier to make her my wife. After we said our "I dos" we went back to our hotel and made raunchy love, like in the movies. I couldn't wait to get home so I could show niggas that what was mine, was mine. I know nobody would have expected this, with all the drama that had been surfacing, but she was Mrs. Sanchez and that was that.

KIA

When Rico sprung this whole marriage thing on me, I couldn't believe it. I didn't think he still wanted to marry me after all that had happened, but he did, so I accepted. I didn't mind eloping either because my nigga was rich, and a wedding would be nothing. Hell, he had bought me a three-hundred thousand-dollar engagement ring. I was not doubting that he would make good on his promise to give me the wedding of my dreams.

I was in marital bliss and didn't take the time to consider the whirlwind of bullshit I had left at home. It was like every time I was with Rico, nothing else mattered or existed. It was like the D'Angelo and Lauryn Hill song in motion. I didn't give a damn about shit. Rico had a way of isolating me, but not in an abusive way. Although this time I had fallen out with my best friend.

That was the only thing that kept bothering me while I was on this mini-vacation. Me and my best friend hadn't spoken in days and although I missed her, I wasn't ready to forgive. But then that was stupid because Rico and I were back together. I had gone and gotten married and the girl that I loved like a sister didn't even know. I felt bad. I decided that once we got back, I was gonna make things right.

The only thing I was worried about was her accepting my apology. We had never had a fight like this. I had never spoken to her like that and I had never accused her of disloyalty. That was one of her pet peeves, for someone to question her loyalty. She had cut a host of people off, family included, and personally, I didn't think I was exempt. I felt it in the pit of my stomach, the fear, anguish and regret. I feared how she would react if I tried to mend things and I regretted that I even said that shit now. How much of a hypocrite was I to walk out on my friend, but end up right back with the nigga I walked out on her for helping get me back? Then I married him!

I couldn't live with myself if I had really lost my friend over this. I had to think of something to get back in her good graces because she had been nothing short of a sister to me since I met her.

"Rico, let me ask you a question," I prompted him once he came from the bathroom.

"What's up baby?"

"How did that whole thing with Jas end up happening anyway? Did you ask her to call me over?"

"Yeah," he shrugged.

"And she just said yeah?"

"Yeah, basically."

I could tell the way his eyes shifted around that he was lying or hiding something. I swear if Jas didn't take me back and I found out that he had something more to do with my friendship ending, it was gonna be hell to pay.

CHASE

I was with my precious little baby Lola while her mother continued to taunt and stress me. She loved testing my patience. I allowed it for the time being because I had hurt her immensely, and I wanted to show her I was sorry by giving her some space. But hell, it had been over two months since Lola had been born and her six weeks were long over. I needed something from her to ease my stress a little, but I was too scared of her response to even ask.

She had brought Lola over to the house I grabbed a few weeks ago. I decided to stay in Detroit a little while until I got my brother out of prison and all the shit between him and Marcus was resolved. She brought her ass over to my crib lookin' so fuckable I literally had to walk out the room to keep from touching her and getting cursed out.

"Chase, come get her, she's crying," Isabella called from the front room.

I quickly came to check on my baby. Isabella had taken off her coat while she was getting Lola situated and checking around my house to ensure it was baby-proofed. She had on this tight-ass tan bodysuit that fit her like a glove. Her body had completely returned to normal and it was eating me up not to be able to fuck her whenever I wanted. I tried not to even look, but she kept bending over to check the wall sockets and I couldn't resist.

"Everything up to your standards?" I asked as she finally stood back up.

"I guess." She rolled her eyes and frowned at me.

"It was good to see you too," I chuckled at her attitude.

"Wish I could say the same."

"So, this how it's gonna be? We just never gonna try and talk things out?"

"Oh, shut up nigga, you ain't tryna talk, you tryna fuck. I see your eyes. I know you," she scolded me.

"Really? Come on, baby, it ain't even that serious."

"Oh, it ain't?" She folded her arms and scoffed at me.

"You know damn well what I mean."

"Nah, I don't."

"I mean you know I wanna fuck, but that ain't all I want, and it's never been all I wanted. I want *you*, all of you. I want our family, together. Stop tryna play me."

"Sucks," she said snidely, staring at me like she didn't give a fuck.

"How long you plan on keeping this up? I'm not gonna wait on you forever. I have needs."

"Yeah, I know. You need yo' dick sucked and them saggy-ass balls drained, right?"

"Stop talkin' to me like that," I warned her.

Insults or not, she was talkin' that shit I wanted to hear, and I was not for being teased.

"Or what?"

"I'm tryna save you baby," I smirked as I stared her down.

"Save me from?"

I started inching closer to her. My dick was solid and stuck out in my gray joggers.

"This dick, now quit playin' before you get me started."

"Keep yo' ass away from me," she challenged as she changed her stance.

I walked up on her, accepting said challenge.

"Or what's gon' happen?" I said when I got close enough to her face to talk directly in her ear.

"I'm not the one making threats. You so mad that you have to suffer some consequences, you been angry for the past two weeks."

"So? I gotta walk around wit' a hard dick all day cuz my bitch still wanna punish me for some shit I apologized and suffered for already. You bein' very unfair."

"You are out of your fuckin' mind, Chase Greene," she said with a wicked laugh.

"Listen, I will never, ever even go near yo' neck again, baby please forgive me," I begged like a weak-ass nigga.

Then she just grabbed my face and slid her tongue down my throat. I pushed her against the wall and kissed her back. My hands started roaming all over her perfect body, from them big beautiful titties to that fat, juicy ass. I was almost there, until Lola started crying. *Fuck!* Isabella saw that as a way out and immediately started putting on her hat, gloves, and coat with a big smile.

"Wait, where you goin'? I tried to stop her while simultaneously pacifying a screaming Lola.

"Bye, Chase," she waved as she darted out of the door.

Angry wasn't the word, but I quickly cooled down at the sight of my beautiful little girl. She stopped crying as soon as I started patting her back and cooing at her. Her smile was so loving and genuine, just like her mom's used to be. Lola was a spitting image of Isabella, and a constant reminder of what our love had created. Words couldn't express how proud I was of the little bundle of joy I now had the responsibility of raising. I was gonna do right by her and that would first have me to do right by her mother.

4

A NOT SO WARM WELCOME

TRE

It was like deja vu. I was getting out of prison again the same way I did last year. It was under the same pretenses and all. The only thing that had changed was the fact that my snake-ass brother, Marcus wasn't here this time. He had gone missing and I knew why. He wasn't ready to face my wrath. He was right to avoid me because with the mind-state I was in, I would have caught a body off my own blood.

My dad, Rico, and Chase were all there to greet me and the love was evident. They were happy as hell to see me a free man again.

"Boyyyy," Rico said as he smacked hands with me.

"Mannn," I said back as I greeted my brother and dad.

I jumped in the ride and we took off, straight toward my house. It was business as usual and I was ready to get home and get in some pussy. Only thing was, I didn't have any to get into. Jas wasn't fuckin' wit' me at all, none whatsoever. She hadn't answered a call, a letter, or a message from my brother or Rico. She was done wit' my ass and I was hurt about it.

"So, Jas still ain't fuckin' wit' me?"

"You still on that? It's a dub, my nigga," Rico told me, laughing at my pain.

"But don't worry, we got some hoes for you," Chase added, tryna console me.

I didn't want hoes, I wanted Jas' hoe-ass.

"Man, fuck that. I want my bitch."

"Well nigga, your coming home party is tomorrow. The word is out, so maybe you'll see her," Rico threw in.

I doubted she would come if she knew it was for me.

"What you need to focus on is money and reconciling with your damn brother," my pops finally cut in.

I knew he was comin' wit' the bullshit. I didn't wanna hear that shit right now. I wanted what I wanted and that was Jasmine.

"I know that Pops, but you know I need to get right. Can't get right without pussy."

"It's plenty of pussy out here, boy. Don't get caught onto one like that's the last. God ain't stop makin' good pussy when he made hers," my pops spat and we all bust out laughin'.

That nigga could make any situation hilarious. I was still gon' do what I had to do to get my girl back, so that shit he was talkin' went in one ear and out the other. He kept the car laughing until I made it home. I bid my family a good night and made my way into my house to get rested up.

I couldn't wait to shower and lay in my California King after all that time I spent in a prison cell. I stayed in the shower for about an hour, and half of it was spent jackin' my dick off to thoughts of Jas. I really missed her bouncin' on this muhfucka like a madwoman. Nobody fucked me like her, not even her hoe-ass cousin. Jas was a different type. The type I loved breakin' down. I silently prayed she would be at my party tomorrow cuz I needed to see her. If she wasn't there, then I would surely be at her doorstep when it ended.

JASMINE

Isabella had been at my house all day begging me to get fine and go to some party with her. She said Chase was gonna be there and this was part of her revenge plan. I still couldn't believe she was holding out this long and not taking him back. It had been well over two months. But in the spirit of hurtin' niggas, I was down for it. A bitch could use a night out. We both had been moping around, being mad and hateful toward niggas for weeks now.

"What you wearing?" Isabella asked me as she pranced around half-naked.

"Girl, nothin' special," I responded a little irritated.

"Bitch, get bad!" Isabella yelled, smackin' me on the ass.

"Bad, or bad-bad?"

"Bad-bad, we got feelings to hurt tonight."

"No, you got feelins' to hurt. I'm cool."

"Girl, whatever. Just put on some short shit. We need to look like heauxs tonight," she raved as she danced around my room.

"Booty shorts and thigh-highs?" I asked, pulling out this ignorant-ass rhinestone-studded two-piece shorts outfit from my closet.

"Yasssss, bitch," she added before whipping out a peach two-piece short-set.

It was cold as fuck outside, but you know the saying: "heauxs don't get cold."

After we got dressed, we couldn't stay out of the mirror looking at our plump backsides and perky titties. That baby had done Isabella justice. Her ass was fatter, and her titties were fuller. Her stomach had no stretch marks and it was flat as before. She had her blonde hair hanging in wispy curls that framed her face. Her makeup was slayed, and her clothes made her curves jump out.

I looked a fine-ass glittery mess. Everything down to my boots was glistening and I was ready to be in the spotlight, makin' heauxs jealous and niggas' dicks hard. I had dyed one lock of my hair honey-blonde while the rest was black, and it was wand-curled in loose waves.

"We is badddd!" Isabella hollered as we grabbed our things to leave.

"We is!" I chimed in, happy I took her up on her offer.

She brought out the silver Benz tonight and we made our way to whatever party she had picked. Once we got there, I became suspicious at the long line. I was not about to stand outside in the cold for nobody. I started to wonder whose party it was to be bringing this type of crowd, but I was buzzed and ready to shake my ass on somebody, so I said fuck it when she pulled into valet.

We cut the line and went in, as usual. I could barely get in the door before niggas was touchin' and grabbin' me tryna get my attention. I kept behind Isabella as she guided us through the thick crowd that had formed on the dancefloor. We found our section in VIP and everybody was there, even Kalief and Simone who I hadn't seen or heard from in a while. But imagine my fuckin' face when I saw Tre standing there drinking a bottle of Dom. I wanted to run, I wanted to puke. I wanted to beat my cousin's ass so bad!

I was frozen for a minute. His eyes met mine and we both just stared at each other. His were shooting love arrows, but mine were shooting daggers. I couldn't believe she set me up, but maybe it was karma for luring Kia to my house for Rico.

"Really, bitch?" I whispered in Isabella's ear when I finally took my eyes off Tre.

"Chase is gonna be here. This has nothing to do with Tre," she lied.

"Girl, fuck you, okay?"

"No, seriously, don't be like this. You know I wasn't trying to set you up. So, don't start acting crazy."

"Wait 'til we get home," I threatened her.

"Just get drunk and make that nigga regret doin' you bold," she urged giving me two shots she snatched off the table.

I gulped them down and she kept them coming. Before I knew it, I had lost my attitude and the ass-shaking had commenced. Then I saw Chase walk in and Isabella turned into a stone-cold freak-heaux. I had never seen no ass shake like the way hers was. I was cackling inside as I watched Chase almost stumble tryna keep his eyes on her and speak to his brother and friends. I decided to be petty and stir some shit up since my cousin thought it was safe to play with me.

I walked over to Chase and gave him a hug. He smiled back at me.

"What's up, Jazzy?" he asked as his eyes traveled over to Isabella's ass.

"Nothin', cousin, how you feelin'?" I asked, joining him as I turned to survey Isabella with him.

"I'm hot, and I know y'all two evil muhfuckas up to something.' I see it all in yo' face."

"Me? No way. As you can see, your baby mama loves setting people up." I referenced her bringing me here in the first place.

"Why she over there actin' up like I won't take her ass in the nearest bathroom and wreck her shit, though?"

"You mad?" I taunted him.

"I ain't gon' lie, that shit burnin' me up right now," he admitted.

"Go get her then," I suggested, nudging him in her direction.

"Man, she gon' go off if I come near her. She drunk? She might be a little friendlier."

"As fuck, go head," I said preparing for the showdown.

TRE

When I laid eyes on Jasmine wit' that fuckin' Selena Quintanilla outfit on, my dick got solid instantly. When she looked back at me, I saw all the hurt and anger in her face. She was not fuckin' wit' me at all and I was mad about it. As I watched her get drunker and drunker, I was waiting for her to forget that she was mad at me so I could at least speak to her, but she kept her back turned as she danced and popped her fat-ass to the beat.

I mean, having that view wasn't bad but damn, I wanted her to at least give me a head nod. Instead, she went and jumped in Chase's face as soon as he came in the booth. I was on fire as I sat there with my eyes glued to her, making sure she wasn't flirting. She wasn't; she was just stirring up drama with him and his devil of a baby-mama, Isabella. I had to say that bitch snapped back after her pregnancy. Whatever genes they had in their family must have made perfect bodies cuz both of theirs were remarkable.

My eyes were silently calling Jasmine as she bent over and bounced her ass up and down, occasionally lookin' back at me to make sure she had my attention. She did. She was all I could see. She was teasing me so bad I just wanted to get up, snatch her, and put her on my dick. I knew my brother was goin' through it as well. Those two bitches came here with torture on their minds. I didn't know what exactly had transpired between Chase and Isabella, but from the eavesdropping I did while he spoke to Jas, I knew she wasn't fuckin' wit' him either.

It sucked for both of us to have the two baddest chicks here and couldn't even touch or talk to them. I was gettin' hella irritated. I was happy that my nigga, Rico had finally arrived and took my mind off the bullshit for a second. What I didn't expect was Jasmine's reaction when Kia went to speak to her.

JASMINE

I was throwin' it down until I caught two familiar light-skinned muhfuckas out the corner of my eye making their way into the booth where we had convened. It was none other than Kia and Rico, smiling and holding hands. I couldn't believe my drunk-ass eyes. I was determined not to even look because I was already on edge and I was drinking. That was a recipe for disaster. I just turned back around and continued to shake my ass. Shit, it had thrown my twerk all off but I still swayed my hips despite all the tension that had filled the room. Then I felt someone behind me. This bitch had the nerve to put her arm around me.

"Bitch, get yo' fuckin' hand off me!" I swiped her shit right off my shoulder.

"Jasmine don't do this here." She got in my face when I turned around.

Was this bitch challenging me? It sure felt like it, so I pushed her ass right out my fuckin' face. She stumbled but her bitch-ass boyfriend Rico caught her. He glared at me so angrily, but I didn't give a fuck. I would fuck both of them up. That bitch already knew what was good.

"So, you really gon' act like this?" Kia collared me by my shirt and pressed her body into mine.

"Bitch, get yo' fake ass out my face!" Nobody touched us cuz we weren't even fighting. We were just grabbing each other, trying not to throw no punches.

We both had hands but the way I was feeling, I would ruin my best friend's face for at least the next six months of her life, if she lived.

"I swear to God if you hit me, Jas, it's over," Kia warned me. She knew I was getting mad enough to do it.

"Kia, get yo' fuckin' hands off me. It's already over. It was over when you questioned my loyalty. It was over when yo' bitch-ass boyfriend put a gun to my head and you accused me of setting you up! So, I'll repeat it for you, since you used to be my bitch, get your hands off me before I break yo' shit, Kia."

"I wanna fuck you up so bad right now." Kia let me go but still pressed her body into me.

She was bigger than me but not by much. I would've tossed her ass right over that fuckin' railing if I had to.

"Fuck *me* up? Not Rico? *Me*? You did that already, Kia. I'll never make another friend as long as I live."

"Y'all just come to the bathroom, we can talk this out," Isabella chimed in, grabbing both our wrists and pulling us toward the stairs.

"Nah, fuck this dick-brained bitch!" I spat as I snatched away from Isabella.

"Nah, fuck you bitch!" Kia yelled back, pushing me in the chest.

I couldn't help it. I swung so fast I didn't realize it until Rico quickly grabbed Kia and got between us. He got in my face and threatened me.

"Hit my wife if you want to," he said with a menacing scowl.

"*Wife?*" I asked as I burst into laughter.

"Yep." He smiled like the devil.

"Bitch, you married this nigga?" I yelled past him and at Kia. "Move Rico before I knock the light-skinned off yo ass. I pushed past him and charged at Kia.

Then he grabbed my arm and yanked me back hard as fuck. My neck snapped in his direction. The feeling in my arm was momentarily gone, that's how fuckin' hard he grabbed me. I hit him so fast his eyes bucked. Then I heard Tre behind me.

"Nigga, I wish you would touch her," he stated calmly to Rico.

"What nigga?" Rico countered.

"Nigga *I WISH YOU WOULD TOUCH HER,*" he repeated.

"Fuck you, Jas," Kia yelled at me and that was it.

I ran up on her but before hands could connect, I was being snatched up by Tre and thrown over his shoulder. We were going toward the exit and I was kicking and screaming. I wanted to beat everybody's ass. Kia, Rico, Tre and Isabella coulda got it.

"Tre put me down," I begged as he got closer to the exit.

"Shut up," he barked as we finally got outside.

The rest of the crew was right behind us, including that bitch, Kia. Tre finally put me down so I could wait for valet to bring the car.

"Jas, you really gon' do me like that?" Kia yelled as she stormed out of the club.

"You lucky I didn't hit you bitch," I spat as I turned my back toward her.

"Ladies, y'all both need to relax. Kia, back up, cuz if you touch my cousin, I gotta beat yo' ass too, boo," Isabella chimed.

"Ain't nobody gon' touch her," Rico yelled over the crowd.

"Nigga, shut yo' hoe-ass up! Dro was just fuckin' that bitch two weeks ago," Tre said to Rico.

Everybody got quiet. I couldn't even say nothing else. That was the haymaker. By then, the car had arrived. Isabella and I hopped in and Tre closed my door and walked to his car which was behind ours. I drove home, and three cars pulled up behind me. It was Tre, Chase, and Rico. Everybody hopped out at once and I feared somebody was gon' die tonight.

Tempers were flaring as they all decided my house was the spot for round two. I was still buzzed and all I wanted to do was go inside and lie down, but with Tre rushing toward me, well everybody, I prepared for the worst.

I fiddled around for my keys and opened the door. Tre barged in and everyone else followed. He took command over the conversation.

"So, this how y'all muhfuckas act when a nigga get home from prison? But y'all supposed to be my people?" He seemed genuinely hurt by the goings on.

"Nigga, you been locked up. You don't know what's been happening since you been away, but that comment you made my nigga, that was some hoe shit," Rico huffed.

"You right, it was, but since when you start getting physical with women? And mine on top of that?" Tre asked.

"I'm not yours," I muttered from the left of him.

"Jas, shut up. I'll deal with you in a minute. But what the fuck goin' on with my family?" He threw his hands up in frustration.

"Well, let's start with the fact that this psychotic nigga came to my house and forced me, at gunpoint, to call Kia over to get his ring back." I hadn't spilled that part yet and I could tell by the look on Kia's face she was shocked.

"Is that true, Rico?" Kia looked at him in disgust.

All he could do was the typical fuck-nigga face-palm.

KIA

When Jasmine's words hit me, I couldn't believe my fuckin' ears. By Rico's reaction, she wasn't lying either. I was disgusted and upset that he had done some shit like that. Then the fact that I had gotten mad at her about that and it was his fault. Then I went and married the fuckin' snake and he didn't even tell me how it happened. He just allowed me to be mad at my best friend cuz he knew I wouldn't approve of him pullin' no gun on her.

I knew Rico was crazy, but for him to do that to Jas was new. I didn't like the way he was acting. That wasn't love, that was some pure psycho shit. It was no telling what he'd do to me if he could do that to Jasmine and she wasn't even the one doing him wrong. I had to rethink this whole marriage thing because right now, I didn't trust his mental stability. I was saying that as if we weren't already married. I had even sent the papers off.

"Jas, I'm so sorry." I ran to her and I was surprised she didn't throw me off her.

She grabbed my arm and dragged me to her room. I could still hear them talking.

"You wanna show me you sorry, bitch?" she asked as she threw on a pair of black Timberland boots.

"Yeah, but what you doin'?"

"I'm finna beat yo' husband's ass. You wit' it or am I gon' have to beat yo' ass too?"

I wasn't scared, but I agreed. Rico needed his ass beat.

"Yeah," I responded as she handed me a pair of wheat Timbs.

Rico deserved it. I had blown up on the only friend I damn-near ever had because of him.

"You know he choked me? He put his fuckin' hands on me, Kia. He held a gun to my head and made me call you over. He scared me so bad that I did it. I didn't know who the hell Rico was, and I was not about to play with my life."

Her words cut me like a knife. I felt so disloyal and treacherous. I laced up the boots and we both stormed back into the living room where everyone stood, still talking and both of us ran up on Rico. We both punched and kicked him.

"Dog, what the fuck?" I heard Tre yell as Rico crashed to the floor from the impact.

Then he swooped Jas up and Chase grabbed me next.

"Let me go, I'm gon' kill that bitch!" Jas screamed from Tre's arms.

She tussled around with him while I found it impossible to get loose from Chase. Rico had collected himself from the floor and he was bleeding everywhere. Jasmine was struggling so hard to get loose from Tre.

"Pleaseeee, please let me go," she begged but he wouldn't.

"Nah, leave it alone," he told her.

"Tre, get yo' bitch-ass off me. You ain't no better than him. You did the same shit and worse!" she screamed, clawing at his arms.

Then she elbowed him in the mouth and made a mad dash toward Rico who was caught off guard again. She started punching and kicking him again until Tre grabbed her. This time, he took her in her room and slammed the door.

"Dog, what the fuck is wrong wit' you?" was all we heard before it sounded like shit started being broken.

I knew Tre wasn't gonna hurt her, so we all left. It was a tiring night. I went my own way cuz I didn't want to be around Rico tonight.

I was sick to my stomach with grief about how he had treated my friend, plus I was scared cuz I had stomped his ass.

I power-walked to my car and got the fuck on. I wasn't going home, and I didn't want to go back to my apartment, so you guessed it, I called Dro. When he didn't answer, I decided to go over there anyway. On the drive, I tried to psych myself out. I took my ring off and put it inside the console. When I got there, I used my key to let myself in.

I heard him in the kitchen. I heard moaning in the kitchen. I peeked my head in and got the shock of my life when he had some bitch on the counter giving her the best dick of her life.

"Dro?" I called as I approached.

"Oh, what's up Kia. This Cookie. She took yo' spot while you ran off wit' yo' bitch-ass boyfriend," he said as he continued fucking her like I wasn't standing there.

I ran up on him and attacked. The girl jumped down and started putting on her clothes. He pulled up his Tommy boxers scowling at me for interrupting his nut. The girl had snuck her ass out the front door.

"Look what the fuck you did! Now you gon' have to finish me off." He laughed as we wrestled around.

"Bitch, I'm not finishing shit, you fuckin' freak-ass hoe. How long you been fuckin' that skinny, white bitch?" I screamed. I was livid.

"For about ten minutes until you interrupted." He looked down at his watch.

"Glad yo' nasty ass used a condom," I spat, pushing him in the chest.

"You the only one who get this muhfucka raw." He bit his lip while grabbing on his dick. "Come on, you finna let me get this nut."

"Nigga, no," I jerked away.

"Girl, get yo' stupid ass to my room." He smacked my ass then grabbed my neck and walked me up the stairs.

He took his underwear off and pulled me into the bathroom with him and into the shower. I barely had on any clothes, so it was easy getting me undressed.

"Yo' why is blood on yo boots?" he asked, surveying my Timbs.

"Long story."

"Tell me," he insisted as he turned the water on and let it get hot.

"I fought Rico. Me and Jas beat his ass," I admitted with my head down.

"Damn," he laughed and pulled me into the water.

He wasted no time locking lips with me. I missed him. I hadn't spoken to him since that shit went down at Jas' house. I knew he missed me too because he didn't put up a fight. He was happy I came over. I felt crazy for fucking him after the scene I had just witnessed, but oddly, I was turned on. I felt Dro kissing the back of my neck as he palmed my ass with both hands. Then he slid inside me, and I swear it was everything I had been missing.

"Mmm, baby, I missed this shit," he moaned as he pounded me roughly.

I bent over and grabbed my ankles, letting him have his way with me. I felt the hot water rushing down my back as Dro slammed into me like he hadn't had pussy in months. It felt so good I came prematurely as fuck.

"Damiennnn, I'm finna cummm," I shouted as he went full force.

"Yeah, cum on that dick," he urged as he slapped my ass.

I don't know why it felt so good, but I couldn't get enough.

TRE

"Everybody left," I told Jas as I peeked outside her bedroom door.

"Well, you should go too," she shot back after ransacking her room trying to fight me.

"Man, no! We need to talk. I'm not leaving here until you listen to me."

"There is nothing to talk about. I am sincerely grateful that you had my back and all, but that's where it ends. You tryna protect me from Rico and you did the same thing he did. You are a hypocrite," she barked.

"Jasmine, listen. I love you, okay? You've been nothing short of perfect since we met. You have no idea what I've been through over the past two years dealing with your cousin. If you can't understand how it looked from my viewpoint, it's because you don't want to."

"You're right, I don't want to," she said, folding her arms and giving me the straight face.

"I know I hurt you, baby, and I'm not making no excuses for my behavior. I should have trusted you, but this is a fairly new relationship. We both caught feelings fast. I didn't know you like that and still don't, but I don't think you would set me up. It just looked crazy and I was so hurt and angry. I'm still growing."

"Well grow with someone else. I'd be a fool to forgive you."

"Jas, please? I'm so sorry and I swear I'll never do no shit like that again," I begged. I had gotten on my knees and hugged her waist as I tried my best to convince her that I was sorry.

"No. Now please leave," she teared up.

I could hear it in her voice that she was about to start crying, which meant she still had feelings.

"Jas, I'm sorry," I said standing up and hugging her small frame tightly.

She didn't fight this time, but she didn't hug me back either. When I finally let her go, I just stared into her tear-filled eyes. My baby was hurt, and it was all my fault. I wanted to make her feel better, so I went in for a kiss. She kissed me back and I felt it, the emotion, the pain, all of it. I palmed the back of her head as I sucked on her bottom lip. My other hand gripped her ass as I pushed my body into hers against the door. I didn't say a word; I was too scared she'd come to her senses and stop me. I slowly pulled her shorts down. I knew she had to be horny as fuck. She was drinking, emotional, and I know nobody touched that pussy while I was gone. Nobody better not had.

I carried her over to the bed and laid her down. I just wanted to suck her pussy 'til she fell asleep. I put my face in it and went crazy. By her reactions, I could tell she missed me.

"Oh my God," she gasped as I sucked her clit and squeezed her thighs, making her unable to move.

I kept sucking until she was pushing my head away tryna run, but I held her still and kept going.

"Pleaseeee, Tre," she called out, but I ignored her.

I had a point to prove and it was that I was the only nigga that could make her feel like this. Her orgasms were powerful the way her body convulsed beneath me. This girl was trying everything in her power to move my head, but it was a no-go.

"Stop stopping me," I mumbled as I continued to slurp on her pussy.

Her head fell back onto the pillow as she released another

orgasm. She came on my tongue as I used my index finger to stroke her clit. I finally felt like she'd had enough because I kept seeing her eyelids flutter and her body was lifeless. I climbed between her legs and kissed her to wake her up. She started rubbing my back while my lips trailed down to her neck. She grabbed my dick that was hard as Chinese arithmetic and started to stroke it. I knew she wanted this muhfucka.

"You want some dick, baby?" I whispered in her ear.

"Yessssss," she said in a barely audible moan.

She was so open and vulnerable, just like I loved. I took off my clothes and repositioned myself between her thick thighs. I eased in slow and the gasp she let out told me that this was everything she needed. I made love to her slow but rough. I pushed my dick so deep inside her, her eyes bucked.

"Damn, I missed you," I proclaimed as my mouth met hers with sweet kisses.

"I missed *you*," she moaned as I sped up my pace.

"Baby, why you do this to me?"

"Do what," she said, looking into my eyes.

"Make me fall for you then break my heart?"

"Tre stop," she begged me as my strokes got rougher and harder.

"Nah, tell me why you did this shit," I barked as I pinned her legs back.

"I didn't do shit," she cried as my strokes became unbearable.

"Yes, you did. You knew what you were doin' when you put this good-ass pussy on me the first time. You knew I was gon' fall for you, but that was all part of the plan, right?"

I made her turn over on her stomach so I could smash that ass from the back.

"Babyyyyyy," she shouted as I fucked her lights out.

"Baby what?"

"I'm sorryyyyyy."

"Oh, now you sorry? How come you ain't write me or take my calls?"

"I was mad," she whined as I choked and pounded her ass out.

"You not allowed to be that mad at me."

"But, Treeee."

"But Tre what? You heard what I fuckin' said!" I slapped her ass with all my might and she squealed and whimpered beneath me.

"I said I'm sorry."

"I don't give a fuck. I can't believe you did me like that, Jasmine."

"I can't believe you did me like that!" She yelled back. "Ahhh, shit!" she screamed out.

She was cumming and I was too.

We collapsed in a sweaty heap and just laid there. She scooted over like she didn't wanna be touched. Hell, I didn't either. It seemed like we were both mad at each other. I realized she was madder because the next morning, I woke up to a note that she was leaving and wouldn't come back until I was gone. Well, at least I got some pussy.

5

BREAKUP TO MAKEUP

CHASE

"Isabella, stop fuckin' playin' man," I screamed into the phone. "I already told you what was up. I don't know why you think I'm gonna change my mind."

"So, you really want it to be over? You really done wit' me, huh?"

"I told you I needed time and that I don't want to be with you right *now*. You can't give me some space?"

"Yeah, but I need some pussy first. If not, shit finna get real ugly for you baby," I threatened, and I was not joking.

That's exactly how I did my ex-wife. Whenever she wanted to cut up on me or disappear, I would find her ass and bring her home. I didn't give a fuck whose house I had to run up in or whose door I had to kick down, I bet I left wit' my bitch. Isabella didn't know who she was fuckin' with and I know I seem a little crazy, but bitches liked that shit, or they wouldn't have stayed. I knew Isabella was trying her best to get under my skin and it was working, so I had to think of a way to get under hers.

I knew she was goin' out tonight with her cousin, so I was about to see what I could do to get some whereabouts out of Jas. I popped up at her house where I had stayed until I found a house of my own. I rang the doorbell and she came and answered.

"What's up, cousin."

She smiled and let me inside. "What's up with *you*? Isabella is not here."

"That's cool. I see you getting ready to go somewhere tonight, huh?"

"Yeah and that's your business?" she joked.

"Is Izzy gon' be with you?"

"Yeah, why?"

"Where y'all goin'?"

"Don't worry about it," she taunted me.

I hated that about both of them. They loved fuckin' wit' niggas emotions.

"So, you gon' let that shit slide that she pulled at the party the other night? Her setting you up and shit?"

She looked at me like I was right. I knew she wanted to get Isabella back for that.

"Don't tell her I told you shit."

And just like that, I had the information I needed. They were gonna be at some fashion event in midtown and now, so was I. I rushed home to get ready. I threw on a cream sweater with some light-blue jeans and some cream Gucci loafers. I had on a small diamond chain and a watch. My cologne could've gotten me the pussy just by the scent. I didn't over-do it. I was casual but fly.

I drove to the venue and ended up paying extra to get in since I didn't have a ticket. When I got inside, I found a seat and sat down. I texted Jas to let her know I was here and to deliver Isabella's ass right next to me. She sent me a confirmation that they were walking in and I sat there, preparing for the awkward look on her face. But, I guess I was gonna be the one feeling awkward when they both walked in with other men. I was fucking livid. I sat there huffing, puffing, and scowling as she pranced in and sat directly next to me with her whack-ass date.

I saw the wicked smile she had on her face. They had planned this. I was ready to act the fuck up, but I had to think on my toes as not to disrupt the event and embarrass anyone. In a minute, I wasn't gonna give a fuck. This nigga had the nerve to put his hand on her thigh and I swear I almost lost it.

"On God, Isabella," I whispered in her ear as she sat there gloating about how pissed she had me.

Then she caressed his hand and that was it.

"Yo, let me talk to you for a minute," I said out loud.

The nigga she was with had the nerve to look over at me like I was crazy. This nigga didn't know who I really was. They both looked at each other and laughed.

"Chase, leave me alone, thanks, I'm trying to enjoy the show," she shut me down smoothly.

I turned my eyes back to the stage and I had to admit, it was some fly shit walking down the runway. I ended up enjoying the show myself and after it was over, I trailed behind Isabella and Jas as they made their way to the exit.

"Let me holla at you real quick," I said as I grabbed Isabella's arm that was interlocked with the nigga she came with.

What pissed me off the most was that she was with some white guy. She always told me they weren't her type, now look at her.

"So, this your new boyfriend or some shit? This the nigga you been giving my pussy to?" I accused her loudly.

They both looked at each other and laughed again.

"Oh, the shit funny right? Jas, Tre know you here with another nigga?" I added, trying to ruin her date as well.

It seemed like everybody was in on a joke that I had no idea of the punchline.

"Y'all ain't gon' be laughing when I pop my trunk." I stood there challenging them. "I bet these white boys don't even know what to do with that pussy."

"You damn right, we don't," the one that was with Isabella blurted out.

Then I saw his hand gesture and the way his mouth poked when he talked. These niggas were gay.

"I see what's goin' on here. This real cute," I said as I finally realized I was set up.

"Chase, take your ass home," Isabella sighed and rolled her eyes.

"No! I need to talk to you, alone, naked," I boldly stated as my eyes roamed her body.

"Girl, you betta go let daddy take care of that," Isabella's date blurted out, and I agreed.

"Johnathan, hush," she said, palming her face.

"I'm just sayin' girl." He high-fived the other.

"Chase, I'm busy with my friends."

"I don't care. I really need you. Please baby, just take care of this and I can't promise I'll leave you alone but at least I won't keep stalking you." I shrugged like that made any sense.

"I already told you I needed time."

"Nah, you need some dick. Let's go." I grabbed her arm and pulled her toward my car.

"Chaseee," she whined as I walked her to my car.

"You been drinkin'?"

"Yeah, why?"

"Get yo' drunk ass in the car. I know you ain't drive here."

"No, Jas drove."

I got in and started the engine. We were on the way back to my house. On the drive, I couldn't help but steal glances at her. She was so beautiful, and I truly missed her. She had no idea how much I cared, though, obviously by the way she was acting. When we arrived, I got out to open her door and we both walked into my place. Everything was quiet and clean, like she liked. We took our coats and shoes off and went into my bedroom. We undressed, and I turned on a movie and lay down next to her. I stroked her hair and face and rubbed her booty until we both fell asleep. I didn't even fuck. I didn't even try. Tonight was about showing her that I wasn't in it for sex. It was about showing her I wanted her. Just her.

ISABELLA

The next morning, I woke up to see Chase had made me breakfast in bed. I was truly surprised that he didn't have sex with me. He just let me sleep. That shit irritated me. While yes, I was trying to teach him a lesson, that didn't mean I didn't get what I wanted when I wanted it. But leave it to Chase to try and flip the script on me.

"So, why didn't we have sex last night?" I asked as he sat the tray down on the nightstand.

"Excuse me?"

"Is that not why you brought me here? To fuck?"

"No, that's not why. I wanted to be with you. I wanted to hold you and sleep with you. Besides, you fell asleep. You were drunk and tired, and I wanted you to want this as much as I do."

"Really? Now you're trying to play the consent card with me, Chase?"

"No, I wanted you to want this, not just the sex, but this. Us being together. Why you actin' so savage?"

"Why you acting so soft? Where's the Chase that was fuckin' bitches in club bathrooms and cheating on his wife and shit? You acting like you really wanna be with me, but I've seen the real you. This ain't you."

"Isabella, I have been nothing but good to you, because I actually love you," he stated calmly as he watched me eat my breakfast.

"I'm not tryna hear that, okay?"

"Well, you are. I was there for you through all of the bullshit. I had your back, I hurt people that loved me for you. I broke promises for you."

"You know what? I'm leaving. I don't have time for the guilt trip." I rolled my eyes and got up to get dressed.

"Really? This is what you took from all of this? I'm just trying to repair a broken relationship, and this is all you can say?"

"Bye, Chase. Don't come around me again."

"I have to. We have a child."

"Well then that's all we need to talk about," I replied.

"You know what? Fine. You want it this way, you got it." He threw his hands up and left the room.

I didn't like the sound of that. I knew how Chase could get. His ignore game was strong. I wouldn't know what to do if I lost him for real, but I was still mad. I wasn't ready to give in just yet.

I left in an Uber and went to get my car from Jas' house.

"Girl, give me my keys," I said to her as I saw that smile creep onto her face when she opened the door.

I knew she thought I had given Chase some pussy by that stupid smirk she wore as I walked in.

"So, you fucked him?"

"No, I didn't," I admitted.

"Why?"

"It wasn't me. He didn't even try. He let me go to sleep then woke me up to breakfast. I told him I still didn't want to be together, but this time, he just said okay."

"Well, you finally got what you wanted." She shrugged and bit into a banana.

"This is not what I wanted, bitch." I rolled my eyes as I sat at her kitchen counter.

"Okay, well stop playin' games. You know I'm all for the get back, but that nigga is dead. You like to kill souls, not just hurt them."

"And why shouldn't I?

"The way I been feeling, I can't even give you an answer."

"Right. That nigga deserves to suffer."

"He does. They all do," she said, looking down at the counter.

"You gave Tre some pussy, didn't you?"

"Yep," she sighed and rolled her eyes.

"Jas, really?"

"Yeah, bitch, I was horny than a muthafucka. You know violence turns me on. Plus, I haven't had sex since Tre went to prison. You know I got trust issues, so finding someone new wasn't on my agenda. I been dry for months. I was drunk too."

"Understandable, but keep your fuckin' head in the game. Don't let him back in," I warned.

"I got this."

"You had better or yo' ass gonna be just like the other bitches they disposed of. Don't be like Liyah."

"Girl, please."

"That's what that bitch thought before she fucked both Chase and Tre. Now look at her, dead and gone."

"No offense, but so did you."

"Yeah and I'm currently still with Chase and he's begging me to stay. I'm a different kind of heaux."

"That is certainly true."

"If it's one thing we have in common, it's knowing how to play niggas. Don't forget that shit, Jas. They will get you if you don't get them. Tre is a shady-ass nigga. He fucked his brother's baby mama. That's why he was in prison this last time. Don't underestimate his ability to hurt the people he loves."

"You're right. I got the perfect plan for that nigga," she said like she came to her senses.

"Good, don't be stupid over him. I know he gives you every reason, but don't. It's not worth it."

After our little pep talk that turned into a movie marathon and smoke session, I took my keys and left. I went straight to Chase's house. I was about to get some dick and leave.

JASMINE

Leave it to my cousin to come and snatch my edges. I hadn't had a reality check like that in a while. She was right, though. Tre couldn't be trusted at all. He was to be used and that was it. After sex, I couldn't lay around cuddling and getting attached. I needed to leave after that. I could cuddle with my pillows if it were that serious. I had to protect myself because it was clear the type of person Tre was. He was a reprobate and those, you just couldn't fix.

I was still very much hurt about that shit he did, and the only remedy I could think of was to make him suffer. This had been a truly painful few months. After I got the dick from Tre, I felt better, but I felt better in a sense of I didn't want him as bad anymore. I guess it was just all the pent-up frustration. I was back on my bullshit, so I got sexy and went over to Tre's unannounced. He opened the door eating a sandwich and was taken aback when I stepped in, revealing the nothing I had on under my tan trench coat.

He quickly followed me as I marched through his house and up the stairs to his bedroom. I didn't give him time to talk before I pulled out his dick and spit on it.

"Damn, baby," he said as he rested on his elbows to watch me attempt to make his whole dick disappear.

I sucked and slurped until that nigga was flinching and moaning like a whole bitch. After I was satisfied with the head job I had just given him, I got on top and slowly slid down on his manhood. He was so confused, but I liked it this way. I bounced up and down while giving him eye contact, letting him know I was in control. I was hoping he would cum while I was on top, so I wouldn't have to worry about what he'd do when he took over. I knew Tre had the power to make me say whatever he wanted to hear, and I wasn't here for that.

"Jasmine, slow the fuck down, you gon' hurt yo'self," he moaned like a coward.

"Shut the fuck up and take this pussy."

I kept riding until he finally had enough.

"Jas, get up before I cum," he yelled in a panic, but that only made me go faster and harder.

"Mmm, shit," he yelled out before I felt all his nut inside of me.

I jumped up and went to the bathroom to pee. When I was done, I politely grabbed my shit and left. I went home to shower and pack my bag to go to Toledo for a few days. I had blocked Tre's number, so he couldn't contact me. Before I even got there on the forty-minute drive, I had about three blocked voicemails. Phase one of the plan was already working.

I was going to play the hot-cold game with him until I broke him. He wasn't ready for the shit I had up my sleeve for his ass. With Isabella on the same tip, we were gonna have these two brothers on their knees in no time, as if we didn't already have that. Speaking of Isabella, she was supposed to meet me there so we could have a relaxing weekend and plot some more. But after calling her several times, I guess she wasn't coming, or maybe she was, from Chase's dick.

CHASE

"Yeah, baby, fuck me," Isabella screamed as I pounded her from the back.

She was acting like she hadn't had no dick in years. I was glad she finally came to her senses and let daddy take care of that shit. It wasn't like the dick wasn't still good just because the relationship wasn't. I think that was part of the reason she wanted a break because she knew if I hit that shit, she would be right back in.

"You love that dick, don't you, bitch," I said as I held her hair tightly in my fist.

"Yeah, Chase, damnnnn it's so good."

"Uh huh, see what you been missin'?"

"Yes, baby," she cooed as I softly kissed her neck.

This was the Isabella I missed. The Isabella I had been getting was probably the one her husband and my brothers dealt with. I had always had the sweet one. She loved me before we even met as adults, but lately, I hadn't been getting shit from her but hatred and her being nonchalant. That shit had me feeling all types of ways. I couldn't handle being brushed off by her like I meant nothing. Little did I know, she was about to do it again. Soon as we were done, her ass got up and dipped.

"Why you leavin'?" I asked as she gathered her things.

"I'm meeting my cousin somewhere, I'll see you later," she told me and walked out.

Damn, that was a savage-ass move, but what could I expect? She had more than shown me that she was savage as fuck. She didn't hug or kiss me before she left, and that had me thinking we still weren't back right. I was almost at my breaking point. If she didn't care about this relationship, then why should I? I decided right then that I was done being emotional and chasing her ass. If she wanted this to be over, then it was over. I showered and played video games for about an hour to take my mind off her and that good pussy she had just thrown on me.

My phone started to ring, snapping me out of my depressed-ass thoughts. It was my brother, Tre, so I picked up.

"What's good, bro?"

"Nothin' man and I mean that," I laughed.

"Any idea where yo' baby mama is?"

"Hell if I know. She said she had somewhere to be with Jas, then she left. I don't know what's up with that girl no more."

"Well if you wanna know, they're in Toledo at some spa hotel."

"How you know that?"

"I got this location tracker thing on my phone."

"That pussy don' turned you into a stalker, bro," I asked him.

"Hell yeah, don't act like you don't care what Izzy doin' either cuz yo' ass sure popped up at that fashion show the other day. Jas told me."

"I did. But Isabella been on some straight fuck-shit lately. I don't even know if I care anymore," I admitted, and I felt like I meant it.

"You ain't over her, nigga, don't even play like you are. That's how you lose."

"I already lost. She got me out here like a sucka. Following her and poppin' up and shit."

"Nigga, you did the same with Liyah, God rest her soul. Don't change up now. Plus, I need you to ride out there with me."

"Nope, you're on your own. She wanna leave, she can."

"Nigga, what? Since when you start being passive when a bitch playin' in yo' face?"

"Nigga." I had to laugh at that. He was right. "A'ight, I'll go."

"Good, cuz I'm outside." He laughed and hung up the phone.

This nigga here.

I quickly grabbed a duffle bag and loaded a few things, grabbed my gun, and went to join him on this excursion. We smoked and talked shit the whole way there. They ended up in Maumee, Ohio, but that was only a half hour more, so we kicked back and enjoyed the ride. I couldn't wait to see the looks on these bitches' faces when we got there.

We checked in at the Homewood hotel and I immediately started to ask if Isabella or Jas was staying here. They wouldn't give the information, but then Tre pulled out a ring box and convinced the clerk that he was doing a surprise proposal, she gave him their room number so fast. She was smiling from ear to ear like it was her who was getting proposed to. Once we had the information, we went to our rooms, dropped our shit, then filed back out to theirs.

Tre knocked on the door then we both moved from in view of the peephole. Isabella came and opened the door. The look on her face was priceless as Tre and I barged into the room.

"What the fuck are y'all doin' here," Isabella asked as we started checking the closet and bathroom.

"Y'all got some niggas in here?"

"Other than y'all two idiots, no. Now get the fuck out. We tryna enjoy our weekend."

Jas never looked up from her laptop. I could tell she was mad at Tre, and they needed some privacy, so I dragged Isabella to my room.

"You can't be poppin' up on me like this. How'd you even know I was here?"

"Don't worry about all that, beautiful. Just know I *always* know where my pussy is."

"You're sick, Chase. Get help," she said as she frowned and plopped down on the bed.

"Why y'all at this three-star hotel, though?"

"We just needed a quick getaway that was a short drive. This is actually nice as hell."

"It ain't bad, but you a rich heaux as you call it."

"Nigga, don't get beat up." She laughed and threw a pillow at me.

"But for real, baby, why you dip on me? I thought we was gettin' back right."

"I told you I had somewhere to be. This was it. Jas said she needed to get away for a few days, so we dipped. I can't go nowhere now?"

"Please girl, you ain't even hug or kiss me before you left."

"And," she asked defiantly.

"Then that mean you ain't tryna salvage shit wit' me. You been actin' the fuck up lately, for no reason."

"Have I? Show me what daddy do when I act up," she said lustfully.

I finally got a good look at her eyes. They were red as hell and low.

"Bitch, you high?"

"No, I'm horny," she giggled as she reached for my dick.

"I just fucked you though."

"Nigga, don't blow my fuckin' high with your erectile dysfunction bullshit."

"Bitch, come here."

That was her last time insulting me. That shit made my dick hard as hell when she got all aggressive on that freaky shit. I had her bent over in no time, screamin' my name loud enough for the neighbors to hear.

JASMINE

"So, this what you doin' now right, fuckin' and dippin' huh," Tre asked as he stood next to my bed.

"I have to stay with you every time we have sex?"

"Listen, don't play wit' me, man. You know exactly what you doin' and I don't like that shit at all."

"I really don't give a fuck what you like. I have to keep my distance. I don't want another gun in my mouth unless it's some foreplay shit."

"What the fuck is wrong with you?"

"You."

"Jasmine, cut this shit out. You know damn well you wanna be with me. You can't stay away from this dick and I can't stay away from you at all. Let's both stop."

"I don't know why you think that because you're saying sorry, I'm obligated to forgive you and let you back into my headspace. That shit you did was unforgivable, and I'm not about to be the dumb bitch that keeps forgiving a nigga for doin' fucked up shit to me. If you wouldn't have killed that girl, Liyah, you would have somebody that was with that shit." I let him have it.

"Word?" His whole facial expression changed. I knew he didn't like what I said, but I hardly gave a fuck.

"Word," I said and continued scrolling through my Facebook notifications.

"First off, I didn't kill her. I have never killed a woman in my life."

"Well damn, I was about to be your first. I feel special."

"Jasmine, stop playin' wit' me, man. I was not gonna do that shit. I was just mad."

"Yeah, tell me anything. If it weren't for that call, I wouldn't even be here right now. You know what? I want you to leave."

I hopped up, sat my laptop down and walked to the door to let him out.

"I ain't goin' no muthafuckin' where." He folded his arms defiantly.

"Get the fuck out, please. I can't even look at you right now without wanting to fuck you up."

"Fuck me up then," he offered.

I wanted to so badly. I jumped in his face ready to fight and he didn't back down. So, of course, I slapped the shit out of him. He didn't budge at all. I took the liberty of throwing a mean left hook that caught his jaw and finally caused him to back up a little.

"Oh, now you scared huh?"

"Nah, Jas, do what you gotta do, but just know I'm fuckin' the shit outta you when you finish," he warned, and he was not exaggerating.

After he finished spitting blood, he returned from the bathroom completely naked with a scowl on his battered face that shook my entire soul. Externally, I showed no fear, but I was cowering on the inside. I just knew this nigga was about to try and kill me with that lethal dick game.

"You ready? Cuz it's my turn," he said with a grin.

"Tre, just have a seat and relax," I said, trying to calm him but he wasn't tryna hear that shit.

"Nah, stand up, take that shit off, and bend yo' ass over."

"Can we talk for a minute?"

"This ain't no Tevin Campbell song, bitch. Do what I said, or I can get you up myself, however you want it," he said, clasping his hands together.

I reluctantly stood to undress. He watched me like a creep, contemplating how he was about to damage me. I couldn't say I wasn't turned on. The weed had my hormones on a twenty, on a scale of one to ten.

"That's a good girl."

Once I finished taking off my clothes, surprisingly, he pulled me into a kiss. It was soft, passionate and loving.

"I'm sorry, baby. I swear I'll never hurt you, okay," he said into my mouth.

I wanted to believe him but the stubborn side of me just wouldn't allow it. I hated the way I felt about him. I was ready to go back on my word and be a weak bitch just from a kiss. I wished that shit would never have happened. I tried desperately to put myself in his shoes. Would I be ready to kill him had I thought he had set me up multiple times? Still, I couldn't let the shit go. However, the head he had started giving me had its way of temporarily making me forget the pain.

6

DO OVER

MARCUS

Since that talk with my father, I had kind of eased up on the murderous thoughts about my brother. I hadn't seen him in so long, I started to miss him. I would never admit this to him though, but I still loved him, snake or not. My pops had a way of making me feel like shit with just his glare and that look of sheer disappointment he had whenever he came around. I couldn't stand that shit because all I ever wanted to do was make my father proud.

That's the reason I even picked up a gun and did his dirty work. The reason I became the cold-blooded killer I was today was because I had this need to please my dad. He worked hard to take care of us. He loved my mother and provided for his family by any means and all I wanted to do was repay him for the sacrifices he'd made. In return, it had turned me into a monster, a killing machine with no conscience or remorse. When I caught my first body years ago, I felt like a man. Now, I didn't feel shit at all.

At some point, I started to think I needed therapy, but regardless of that confidentiality bullshit those doctors sign, I doubted that I would be willing to go into some mental health clinic and tell some random stranger that I was a killer for hire and not expect them to go to the police. So, I kept all that shit to myself although I desperately needed to talk to someone about it. I started to talk to myself about it and ended up feeling like the dude from *Split*. Maybe I did need to talk to my father and reconcile with my brother, but pride wouldn't allow it.

I was at the hospital checking on one of my partners that had gotten robbed and shot while he was delivering product. Actually, I was there to finish the job. That nigga didn't seem too solid after that and I couldn't risk a snitch in my camp. I crept into his room and found him sleeping peacefully. Little did he know, he was about to sleep peacefully forever. I stood over him and lightly pulled a pillow from behind him that was propping up his head. I gripped it tightly, pondering if I should do this now or later, when a nurse walked in.

"Umm, what are you doing?" the nurse asked me curiously.

"I was making my boy more comfortable. His neck was crooked," I lied quickly as I tossed the pillow into the guest chair and sat on it.

"Oh, okay, well I'm Jason's nurse, Tiffany," she introduced herself with a smile.

When I finally got a good look at her, I was immediately intrigued. She was gorgeous. Her swarthy complexion was radiant and glowing. Her face was void of makeup and her hair was thick and coiled. Her smile lit up the room while her wide, curvy hips took up my personal space. She was thick in them pink scrubs. Nothing could hide that shape of hers.

"Nice to meet you. I hope you're taking good care of my partner."

"Of course, I am." She smiled wider as she fixed his cover and started to check his vital signs.

"Any updates on his condition?"

"Well, he's expected to make a full recovery. The bullet missed anything important and he should be good to go after a week or so," she said with her eyes glued to her medical equipment.

"You're beautiful," I slipped and said as I stared at her every move.

"Well, thank you. I didn't get your name."

"Marcus," I offered as she finally gave me eye contact.

The way she looked after him made me miss having a woman who took care of me. I used to dog Ava and she was the one who truly cared for me. I had half-a-mind to believe that I was the one who pushed her into the arms of my brother. I quickly took my mind off that scenario and focused back on the beautiful, brown nurse that had just saved Jason's life. I was about to shoot my shot.

"So, what do you do for fun?"

"When I'm not working, I like to volunteer at other nursing homes. They have this program where some of us go and just sit and talk to some of the patients there. They need someone to talk to sometimes, you know," she said, cocking her head to the side.

"Yeah, that's a nice thing to do. I wish I could do something like that."

"You actually can. You can sign up with me." Bingo.

"Can I go with you too?"

"Sure, Marcus," she chuckled knowing I was tryna get on.

"Cool. Maybe we can grab something to eat afterward and I can finally get to know a decent human being."

"Really? So, you don't know any decent humans?"

"If you only knew the half," I sighed and sank deeper into the chair.

"Well, sure then. I want you to see what we do. We touch so many lives and make so many people happy. You know, a lot of older people are lonely and abandoned by their families. Some only get visits from their grandkids so they can make sure they're still dying so they can get their money. It's really sad," she admitted, her face changing to a more somber expression.

"Damn, that sounds awful." I shuddered at the realization.

How shitty would it feel to have your family only come see you because they were waiting for you to die?

"It is. This lady that I go see every week, her daughter bled her dry when she turned over her power of attorney to her the last time she had a stroke. She thought she wouldn't make it, so she signed her rights over, but she ended up living and now the daughter stole all her money. It's a damn shame. The lady is using her last breath to fight to get her money back," she explained.

"Wow. I really want to go now. I would love to help out some of these people. Do you accept monetary donations?"

I figured since I was doing so much fucked up shit out here, the least I could do was a few good deeds to try and offset all the bad karma I know I deserved.

"That would be amazing. I have a list of supplies that are needed for some of the patients. If you are really serious, you have no idea what this would mean to me," she beamed.

She then pulled out her phone and scrolled through dozens of pictures of her with old ladies and men and I had to say, they looked like they were having the time of their life. There were pictures of her painting their nails, dancing, and playing bingo. Even my non-existent heart was warmed looking through her photos.

"Wow, that's amazing. And I'm dead serious. I think I need some good karma in my life, you know?"

"Definitely. So, what happened with your friend if you don't mind me asking?"

"He was just at the wrong place at the wrong time." I shrugged.

"I see. Well, here's my contact information. Please don't get me all excited and then play me. We've gotten lots of people to say they'd help but didn't," she said, handing me a business card.

"If it means I get to hang out with you, I'm there. But let me show you I'm serious." I went into my pocket and pulled out a wad of cash.

It wasn't much, only a grand, but I was tryna show her that I was gonna keep my word. I handed it to her and I could tell she was impressed. Not by the money, but by my willingness to give to her cause.

"Thank you," she said.

Her voice was cracking. She was getting worked up like she was about to cry. And she did. When I saw her hand cover her mouth, I knew the tears would follow.

"No, don't cry." I jumped from my seat and came to her side.

She leaned into me and just kept thanking me. All this time I thought insurance paid for all their needs but the way she talked, some people had more than others.

"Thank you," she said in a whisper. "You're a Godsend."

But I knew I was nothing but the devil.

"No problem, seriously. I just want to help wherever I can. Money ain't never been an issue."

After she finally stopped crying, I wiped her face, hugged her and prepared to leave. Jason would live to see another day.

"So, when is our first date at the nursing home?"

"Is Friday good?"

"Yep. I'll see you then," I said before turning to leave.

KIA

I knew Rico probably thought I was somewhere laid up with Dro, but no, I was visiting my mother and father in Georgia. They kept bugging me to come see them and saying we really needed to talk. I guess they had seen that I was married via social media and were probably upset that they weren't invited. Little did they know, I hadn't even had an official ceremony yet. I honestly didn't know if I was at this point. I was still highly upset with Rico about what he did to my best friend.

When I stepped off the plane, my mom and stepdad were at the airport looking like proud parents. They were acting as if I wasn't the child they didn't like as much. See, Mercedes was the favorite. Namely because my mother was married to her father, and she was the type that did anything for a man, including treating her first child like a stepchild. I hated how Mercedes was treated compared to me. It was like she could do no wrong and everything I did was never good enough.

My face was stern and serious as I approached them. I wanted them to see the disdain I carried for the both of them. The craziest part in all of this was that my stepdad was nicer to me than my own mom. I just didn't like the fact that he never checked her about the difference in the way she treated me versus Mercedes. If he cared as much as he claimed, he would have said something to her, but he didn't, so to me, he was just as guilty as she was.

"Kia, we missed you," my fake-ass mother squealed as I got close enough for her to pull me into a hug.

"That's nice," I remarked snidely.

"Ohhh, don't be that way sweetie," my stepdad, Mark said as he hugged me without my permission as well.

We got into their Audi truck and made our way to their huge house in La Grange. I had to admit, they did well for themselves. My mother owned a floral shop there and my stepdad owned a luxury car lot, so they made good money.

When we arrived, I got out and Mark grabbed my luggage, leading us up the walkway surrounded by a perfectly manicured lawn.

"This house is nice," I stated, my face still holding that lifeless expression.

"Thank you. Your mother picked it out."

Once we got inside, I was ready to immediately turn and leave once I laid eyes on Mercedes. She was smiling from ear-to-ear like we were cool or something.

"Oh, hell no," I screeched and stopped dead in my tracks when I saw her.

"Kia, don't start this mess. You need to act like you're a part of this family," my mother scolded me, pushing me further toward Mercedes who now wore a dumbfounded expression.

"Kia, we aren't sisters? What's the problem? You barely talked to me while I was in Detroit, now you act like you can't even be in the same house as me. Seriously, what's your issue?"

"I don't have an issue. Now where's my room," I asked, snatching my luggage from Mark and stomping toward the spiral staircase that lead to the upstairs bedrooms.

"Third door on the left," my mother sighed as I climbed the stairs with my heavy bag.

I found my room and plopped down on the freshly made bed. I

was not coming out until it was time for dinner. I wasn't in the mood for conversation from any of them after they basically ambushed me into talking to Mercedes. I knew it wasn't totally her fault for the fact that she was always favored over me, but she gloated about it on several occasions. That was the shit I didn't like.

It was like I had to work twice as hard just to get a pat on the back and all Mercedes had to do was simply exist and she was praised like she had discovered the cure for cancer. I hated the way my mom acted toward her like she didn't have another daughter that was with her way before Mercedes even came into the picture. Like, how do you abandon one child for another like you can't love them both equally? Then the names.

My mom named me Kia, like the car, cute right? But Kia's are cheaper and less maintenance. Then she goes and names her Mercedes, a more expensive, foreign, luxury vehicle which just showed how she really felt about me. I was the child of lesser value and importance. I knew it was a huge mistake coming here because I had only been here all of twenty minutes and I was already in my feelings.

I sighed heavily as I unpacked my clothes. I was only staying for a few days and I was already completely drained. It was only going to get worse, so I tried mentally preparing myself for their explanations and half-assed apologies. I envisioned Mercedes' stupid-ass face as they sat there trying to show me that they loved me and weren't terrible fucking parents to me. No, there was no abuse or anything but feeling like you're never good enough while simultaneously always being in competition is mentally and emotionally exhausting.

I sat there for a while longer, sinking deeper into my anxiety when I heard a soft knock on the door. Then I saw Mercedes peek her head inside. My eyes rolled so hard. She was the last person I wanted to see or talk to.

"I was just checking on you," Cedes said as she sauntered in like she was invited.

"I'm fine, you can go." My voice was laced with attitude and resentment.

"Kia, whatever it is you have against me, you can chill now. We grown."

"I don't have shit against you."

"You do, though. You can't stand the sight of me. When I was in Detroit, you barely spoke to me. We are sisters. We shouldn't be acting like this toward each other. It makes no sense." She had sat down next to me and I scooted over because I didn't want to be near her.

"It's not you. It's what you represent. You were and still are the object of your parents' affection. I was treated like I didn't belong. I performed my ass off only to be barely noticed while you sat around doing nothing and got praised like some type of child prodigy."

"So, why are you mad at me and not them?"

"Because there were times where you were happy with the difference in treatment we received. Like you were proud to be privileged, which is one thing, but then you were happy that I wasn't. What type of sister wants to see her sister get treated like that?" I asked, tearing up a bit.

"Kia, I'm sorry okay," she whispered, starting to become emotional.

She knew what I was saying was true. There were many times that she was treated far better than me. There were plenty of times where she rubbed it in my face. What type of family did I have?

"No need to apologize. What's done is done."

"But I want us to be closer. I hate the fact that we don't have that bond like sisters should. We shouldn't be like this."

"It's okay, sis. You have your parents, who love you. You'll be all right without me."

I literally didn't care that Mercedes suddenly wanted a relationship with me. The idea had come and gone long ago when I tried to have this conversation before. There was no getting through to her, so I had said fuck her long ago. I had gotten rid of the notion that we could ever be those type of sisters.

"Kia, please just—"

"No! You don't care, your parents don't care, nobody cares. So, just leave me be. I don't want anything to do with you and sometimes I wish you were of no relation to me. You suck as a sister and as a person in general," I spat.

I knew I was being harsh, but it felt good to be the one being mean for a change.

RICO

This bitch, Kia was still out here playin' games and I was about to play too. She was seeing Dro behind my back and I couldn't take it anymore. I had given her everything she ever wanted only for her to continuously show me why I should have never changed in the first place. I had something for her, though. I had upped me a new bitch, and I couldn't wait to show my wife my new girlfriend.

I had stopped by to visit Kalief because I hadn't heard from him in a while and I needed him to do a job for me. After he had gotten shot up, we gave him plenty of time off the clock to rest and get his mind right. He insisted months ago that he was all right, but I needed to be sure. Aside from the injury, I knew him and Simone were a couple now and she wasn't letting that nigga out of her eyesight. She took good care of him too, and for that, she deserved his undivided attention for a while.

I had also noticed that Simone, Jas, and Kia didn't really hang much anymore. I don't know what transpired between them that caused the split, but it was painfully obvious that something wasn't right. Jas and Kia had barely been seeing each other, at least from what I know. I hadn't seen much of Kia either and that was the main reason I was about to do me. How the hell we married, and I hardly sleep in the same bed with my wife? What the hell kind of marriage was this? I was done with her bullshit.

Once I made it inside of Kalief's house, I took a seat and waited for him to join me in the dining room.

"Long time no hear." Kalief smiled as he walked into the room.

"Who you tellin'? You just went ghost on niggas."

"Mannn, this woman right here be holdin' a nigga hostage 'round this bitch,' Kalief joked as Simone playfully hit him in the shoulder.

"Boy, please. You the one that doesn't wanna go nowhere anymore. Can't stay off yo' knees from eating this p—"

"Baby chill, damn," he said, cutting her off before she told all they business.

"I'm just sayin'," she said before turning to leave.

"What's wrong wit' that girl, dog?" he asked me like I didn't deal with the same unfiltered shit from Kia.

"We deal with some crazy women, you know this. They all cut from the same cloth."

"True true. So, what's the deal? What you need?"

"So, I need your expertise on this new project I'm venturing into. I need you to read over this contract and let me know if it's something I should fuck with or not." I handed him the manila folder I had brought with me.

"I can definitely do that for you," Kalief agreed, scanning through the documents.

"Cool. So, when's the baby shower?" I asked Kalief and he looked at me crazy.

"What you mean, dog?"

"Simone pregnant than a muthafucka."

"Huh?" He genuinely looked confused.

"Do you see her face? That pudge in her stomach? I ain't never seen Simone wit' a pudge nigga."

"She on birth control, though," he said laughing.

"Listen, that girl is pregnant. I have always been able to tell when a woman was with child. Ever since I was a kid, I always knew. One of my aunts who swore she couldn't have kids ended up getting pregnant and I was the first to know. Just check, doesn't hurt to be sure," I told him.

I wasn't lying about that story either. I had some sort of gift when it came to detecting a pregnant woman.

"I sure will."

"You want a baby with Simone?"

"Hell yeah, but I wanna get married first. If she is, I guess we just gon' be doing this out of order, but it'll get done."

"Good shit. So, you wanna marry her?"

"Yep. Ain't nobody else fa' me like she is. It's something about her. She takes care of me and treats me like I fuckin' mean something to her. Unlike that baby mama of mine. You know she been on pure and utter bullshit since I left her, right?"

"Damn for real? That's wild. But man, I wish I had what y'all have." I sighed, thinkin' about how shitty things were between me and Kia.

"Fuck you mean, you got a whole wife," he laughed.

"That bitch don't give a fuck about me. She out here doin' her, runnin' around with that nigga, Dro, still. I thought marrying her chicken-head ass would make shit right, but it made it worse. I got something for her ass though." I was seething just thinking about it.

"Damn, that don't make me excited about marriage."

"Nigga, you got the good one out the bunch. Gon' and marry that girl."

Simone sashayed back into the dining room area and brought us drinks and a plate of hot food. I was so jealous of the thing they had goin' on, but in a good way.

"Oh, and congrats Simone," I said as she was leaving back out.

"Congrats on what," she said, looking confused.

"Yo' ass pregnant," I revealed, scarfing down the broccoli and potatoes on my plate.

"Get yo' homeboy," Simone chuckled, turning to Kalief.

"I don't know babe, yo' stomach is a little pudgy. Maybe you should take a test," Kalief admitted.

"First off, I've been eating more than usual, second I'm on bir—oh shit! I didn't get my shot. *FUCK*," she yelled pacing the floor like a madwoman.

"See," I gloated, knowing I was right.

I finished eating and excused myself while they talked about their new addition to the family.

"Make sure I get a special invite to the shower," I yelled before leaving.

Kalief was too busy comforting Simone to even notice I had left. I had to go because I had more pressing issues to deal with. I mean, maybe if I hadn't done what I did to Jas, Kia wouldn't have been so mad at me. I mean, my own wife and ex-sister jumped my ass. I had to laugh at that shit. They fucked me up too, but I guess that wasn't enough. She just had to keep on fuckin' me up.

7

BABIES AND BULLSHIT

SIMONE

Finding out I was indeed pregnant threw me for a loop. When that test came back positive, I cried for an hour. They were tears of joy, though. I was happy as hell to be carrying my man's baby and he seemed happy too. He was smiling from ear-to-ear and couldn't stop rubbing and kissing my belly. I was three months when I found out that I was with child, and the four months that followed showed me why I couldn't have picked a better man to settle down with.

Kalief showered me with constant attention and affection. He waited on me hand and foot. He went to all my doctor's appointments. He was already showing me he was the perfect father. His daughter was excited about her brother as well. Yes, I'm having a boy and Kalief's daughter, Jayla moved in with us. Her crazy-ass mother, Kema, hated that Jayla wanted to move with us but I didn't give a shit. We were about to be one big family with the new addition we had arriving in two months.

It was time to start planning the baby shower. I wanted it to be huge. I had rented out this space and my event planner, Nori, was hookin' it up. It was gonna be decorated in baby blue, silver and white. It cost me around twenty-five thousand, but I didn't care. It was anything for my unborn. Kalief didn't complain either. He just wrote the check.

After all the invites were sent out and people started to R.S.V.P., that's when I went to get fitted for my dress. It had to be specially made to accentuate the baby bump. It was a long, flowy white gown with silver embellishments. It had a sheer, white train with baby blue fabric layered underneath. I was happy to be having a May shower and a summer baby. Everything was gonna be so beautiful and memorable.

The only thing that bothered me was that I hadn't talked to Jas and Kia in a while. I hoped they would even want to come. I still sent them an invitation, but them being mad at me weighed heavily on my mind. I was still very much in this friendship, but I had to take some time to nurse my man back to health. After that, I found out I was carrying and had been super busy since then. I wanted to be healthy and prepared for when my first child came into this world.

JASMINE

I was back home from another little impromptu getaway I had taken yet again. I just couldn't handle being around Tre for long periods of time. I would disappear every so often to get the space and recovery time I needed. I always, at least, left the state because I wouldn't be able to be alone if I stayed. I still wasn't over him pulling that gun on me and I didn't know when I would be. I wished it had never happened because I really had genuine feelings for Tre, but I just couldn't forgive that shit.

Every time I left, I got a million calls and texts from him. I would end up shutting my phone off or blocking him until I popped back in town. Oddly, the time before this, he was at my door when I got here. My energy levels were low as it was and hearing his nagging every time I wanted some me-time was draining. If he had never done that ignorant shit, we would've been married by now.

Speaking of married, I hadn't seen much of Kia these days. The last time we spoke, she was visiting her parents in Atlanta. Speaking of the devil, she started to call my phone.

"Hey—"

"Bitch, open the door, you not gon' believe this shit," she huffed.

I hurriedly went to my front door and let her in. She had the meanest look on her face.

"Who pissed in yo' coffee this afternoon, bitch?" I stepped aside as she walked in smelling like weed and attitude.

"Look at this shit I got today. Did you get one?"

It was a baby shower invite from none other than our best friend who had been missing in action for months. I hadn't seen or heard from her and by Kia's reaction, neither had she.

"I don't know, haven't checked the mail." I stepped by her and went into my mailbox. It was there.

It was a beautiful invitation and they were having a boy. My nose turned up against my will. If it wasn't for Kalief, I wouldn't even go.

"You goin' to that shit?" Kia asked, snapping her neck all ghetto.

"Yeah. I mean, it is Kalief's baby. That's my family, regardless."

"Yeah, that's the only reason I'm going," Kia said, folding her arms. "I just don't get her. You don't tell your best friends shit about you being pregnant, then you wanna up and invite them to celebrate some shit? This bitch is really crazy."

"Well, we know that part. She's still our friend and you know what happened to Kalief. I was kinda distant when I got shot."

"Kalief got shot, not her," she corrected me.

"But that's her man. You know Simone can be a bit of a pick-me," I said, and we both laughed.

"Her bitch-ass can pick some new friends too."

"Girlll," I squealed as I bust out laughin.'

Kia was not happy at all about this. I wasn't either. I at least expected a phone call or something. She was treating her best friends like some regular-ass associates. I had heard from Kalief more than I'd heard from her these past seven months. We were still gonna show up despite the ill-feelings we had about Simone's disappearing act. Kalief was family, and we always supported family.

I just wasn't ready for all the possible drama and tension this gathering could cause. I know Rico was invited, Tre too, and with what Kia had told me about their marriage being strained, this whole thing had the potential to go left. All the way left. I was thinking kinda far in advance but that's how my mind worked. I knew Tre was gonna think it was all good cuz we were celebrating, but it wasn't. I was still feeling a way about him and it wasn't changing no time soon. I just hoped I could get through the event without having to show my ass, cuz I would.

I sort of wanted things to be over between Tre and me. I was still actively sleeping with someone I shouldn't have been. I should've been too angry and hurt to let him near me, but no. I was droppin' ass every time he came around. There was an undeniable sexual chemistry between us. Why did it have to come at my expense, though? I felt like every time I willingly laid with him, I was sending a different message than intended. I wanted him to know he fucked up and that he had hurt me badly, but I couldn't even keep my composure around him long enough to put my foot down.

Sex is truly powerful and don't let anyone tell you otherwise. Especially with a nigga like Tre. He knows what to do and say to get your defenses down. He's aggressive and dominant, overpowering in a sense. He likes to blame his own lack of self-control on how irresistible you are because he knows that's an ego stroke for most women and a way out of accountability for him. Our little affair should've been over months ago, but it was a different story when we came face-to-face.

Us running in the same circle didn't help either. The likelihood of us crossing paths was high. It was to the point that I almost didn't want to go to Simone's baby shower because I knew he'd be there. Usually I can make sound decisions, but with him knowing my weaknesses, it was damn-near impossible. That coupled with my medication made it worse. He was one of the only people that understood what I'd been through and he still managed to fuck up. It was fuckin' sad that I couldn't muster up the strength to let go. Was I becoming a weak bitch? Find out on the next episode of Dragonball Z.

MARCUS

Tonight, was my first official date with Tiffany's fine ass. We had been texting and talking all week, so I had gotten to know quite a bit about her. She was a good girl but headstrong, smart and not falling for no bullshit. She was soft and feminine but had this edge about herself that let you know she could be just as evil as she was sweet. I liked that about her. It showed me that she wasn't boring and that there was a lot to her to be explored.

She was modest, but flirted a lot. I hoped she was like that in person. I tried to imagine her without the scrubs and how her curvaceous figure would look in a form-fitting dress. My dick stiffened at the thought. It had been a while since I was genuinely feeling a chick. With all the hell I'd been through and caused over these last few years, I wondered what I'd done to deserve someone like Tiffany. She was perfect so far and even with all my bad experiences, I knew a good soul when I felt one.

With other women, it was lust. I mean, I wanted to smash Tiffany and all, but I could wait 'til the second night. Speaking of her, I had pulled up outside her house for our date. I behaved like a gentleman and went to her door to ring the bell. I had brought flowers too. When she came to the door looking beautiful in a simple nude-colored dress with a nude and black, color-block shawl, I smiled a little too hard when I finally saw what was under those scrubs. My heart was beatin' out my chest like a cartoon character.

"Goddamn, Tiff, don't hurt a nigga," I joked.

"I clean up nice, don't I?" she teased, spinning around so I could see all of her.

"Hell yeah," I exclaimed as I escorted her to my car.

"This is nice," she commented, surveying the inside of the car I had just purchased a week ago.

"Not as nice as you in that dress."

She showed me the way to the nursing home we were visiting. When we arrived, everyone's faces lit up. They were so happy to see her, it even made *me* happy.

"Tiffyyyy, you brought a guy?" one of the elderly ladies at the table said as she greeted her with a warm hug.

"Oooh, Tiffany got herself a man," another lady laughed from the opposite side of the table.

"Now you hush, Marie. This is my *friend*, Marcus," she introduced me. "Marcus, these are my lovely ladies Rose, Marie, and Patricia."

"Nice to meet you all." I waved, but they all came to shower me with hugs.

It was so sweet. It felt so good to be surrounded by love for a change.

TRE

I had enough of Jas and her disappearing acts. That shit drove me crazy every time. I hated that she still was so hurt about what transpired between us. I fucked up, yeah. I tried to make it right, it still wasn't. The only person I wanted to be around didn't want to be around me and that shit hurt the most. I wanted her to forgive me, but it seemed like she couldn't. The only thing she did do was give me pussy. I don't think she could help herself when it came to that. But if she could, that would probably stop too.

In the meantime, I had been looking for my brother. It was crazy to me that we hadn't crossed paths yet, even though we ran with the same people. Nobody had seen him except Chase and even he didn't have an address on him.

"Next time you see that nigga, let me know," I said to Chase before hanging up.

I was frustrated trying to get a location on that nigga. I wasn't tryna kill him, I just wanted to *see* him. We needed to *talk*.

Since that wasn't working out so well for me, I decided to put my energy into something else. Mending things. I wanted to show Jas how sorry I was. I realized I hadn't even bought her anything that said I'm sorry.

I went to a floral shop and got her 100 white roses. I also got this oversized card and wrote the longest apology note a nigga like me could muster. There was so much to be said. I made reservations at a nice restaurant and used the rest of the time I had to pray like crazy that she'd accept my invite. I finally worked up the courage to pick up the phone and call her when I was outside her house of course. You can't give a woman too much room in this type of situation.

"Hello," she answered, sounding irritated already.

I didn't care.

"Open the door, please."

I heard her get up and the sound of her feet moving toward the front door. When she opened it, I stood there with the roses and the big-ass card, smiling hard as hell, hoping she didn't slam the door in my face.

"What's all this?" she asked, half smiling.

"This is me saying I'm sorry. May I come in?"

"Sure," she said reluctantly, stepping aside for me to enter.

She gave me a loose hug and I inhaled her scent. She smelled so good.

"You just got out the shower? You smell like heaven," I commented after the hug.

"Yeah. Why so many?" she asked, referring to the roses.

"One for each time I apologize for what I did. I really am sorry, and I hope one day you forgive me, so we can get married or some shit," I shrugged.

She actually laughed this time. I was relieved and happy.

"Thanks, I guess." She nodded, her face still creased from the smile she tried to hold back.

"You gon' read the card?"

"Yes, Tre, I'll read the card."

She opened it and I watched her eyes trail over the words. By the time she reached the middle, I saw tears forming. *Yes!* Inwardly I knew I was getting to her. Once she finished, she was wiping her eyes. She turned to me and just stared.

"Did you mean that?"

"Of course, I did. I wrote it."

"That doesn't mean you meant it."

"I did. I know you're hurt, but it's hurting me more cuz I'm the one that fucked over such a beautiful person. I have never met nobody like you. I finally had the girl of my dreams and look what my dumb ass did. I feel stupid every single day, Jas."

"Tre, I just don't know."

"Take all the time you need, but just know, I'm not goin' nowhere. I'm gonna be here when you finally forgive me, Jas and we gon' live happily ever after."

She giggled at that part. I took the opportunity to grab her chin and kiss her. Her body was tense but the way I caressed her face and held her made her loosen up.

"I can't be doin' this," she said, breaking the kiss.

"Doin' what?"

"Forgiving niggas."

"I'm yo man. Whether you like it or not. I'm done playin' games. Now go get dressed cuz we finna go out."

Oddly, she did what I said. My eyebrows raised in shock as she quietly disappeared to her room and emerged fully dressed thirty-minutes later. She looked sexy as hell in her favorite color, black, the color of her heart and soul.

"Ready?"

"I guess," she murmured.

I grabbed her arm and ushered her to my car. We rode in silence to the restaurant. Once we were inside and seated, I ordered wine and let her do her thang. She always ordered two meals cuz she was greedy as fuck. Whenever I looked at her after ordering she would cut into me with "just mind your damn business."

After the waitress left to put in our food orders, it was time for me to do some more work. I made sure her ass drank enough wine, so she could loosen up. I didn't start talking until she had finished one of her plates. She was always happier when she was full.

"Jas, do you love me?"

She didn't answer immediately. She just stared at me long and hard. I could tell she didn't want to admit it, that she still loved a nigga like me, but her hesitation said it all.

"Baby? Can you answer my question, please?" I stared straight into her entrancing eyes.

I didn't care that I already knew the answer. I wanted to hear her say it.

"Tre, let's not discuss this right now."

I sighed heavily and took my eyes off hers for a moment, only to see the muthafucka I'd been hoping to run into. His snake-ass comes swaggering through this bitch with some woman on his arm and had the nerve to look happy and carefree. How dare he have the audacity to be living his best life while I'm out here struggling to get my woman to admit she even still loved me?

He didn't see me, and I pretended not to see him. After a while, we were finished eating so I wrapped things up. I checked to see how far into their meal they were. Once I saw they were almost done, me and Jas left. We sat in the car and smoked a blunt.

I didn't have to say much to get her to understand what I was up to. She knew what he had done to me. Her only concern was the safety of his date. I assured her she'd be good. When Marcus and his mystery woman finally emerged from the restaurant, my plan was set in motion. I watched as he started the car and took off. I followed him, but not too close.

He had dropped her off then he drove toward the place I was guessing he'd been staying at since I got out. I copied the address and left. I had to plot exactly how I would handle this nigga.

After our date, I was surprised to see I had been put on the block list again by Jasmine. I didn't know what sick game she was playin', but I was muhfuckin tied. She seemed to be all in at dinner, engaging with me and tellin' me with non-verbal cues that she loved me, just to go and block my dumb ass again. It was only so much I could take. I had something for her ass as well.

8

CHALLENGE ACCEPTED

MARCUS

Tiffany had quickly become my favorite pastime. We hung out at the nursing homes for hours, took the residents on outings, and I had no problem helping out financially when it came to the old ladies. Being in that environment was refreshing. I felt different. I was around people that were grateful I was there. It felt good to be appreciated. Now, I still did my bullshit, but Tiffany kept me grounded and gave me a way to balance out the good and evil. We just, clicked. She seemed to really like me, and it felt genuine.

It was week three and we hadn't even fucked yet. That was new to me. I usually hit on the first night and that was it, but I didn't mind waiting. I truly wanted to get to know her. We decided to see a movie and then get takeout and go to my place. Tonight was probably the night, but like I said, I was willing to wait. I enjoyed her company, although I was more than sure I'd enjoy her pussy as well.

"Chinese?" I asked once we left the Black Panther premiere.

"Sure, as long as it's your treat," she giggled.

"It's always my treat, beautiful."

After picking up our food, we headed back to my place to chill. I rolled up a couple blunts without even wondering if Tiffany smoked.

I knew that was most niggas first question to a woman, but I was a little different.

"Do you even smoke?" I finally asked.

"Yeah, boy," she giggled.

We sat there getting high as shit before devouring our food while a movie called "Eve's Bayou" played on my 70-inch TV.

"It's crazy how we been bonding so well over these last few weeks," I remarked, taking my eyes from the screen momentarily.

I grabbed her small hand and she immediately blushed.

"I feel the same. I've been through a lot these past years with dating. I can say you're unlike any of the guys I've been with in the past. I know it's early, but I just get a different vibe from you. You're so sweet and generous."

"Thank you. I'm a firm believer in helping someone that I see is helping others. You got a good heart."

"Yeah? It's my passion. And to find someone who respects that and assists me, it's like a dream come true."

"I'm glad I can be there for you. You know, you've been helping me too. Introducing me to this nursing home shit and just being there for me. I haven't had that in forever. I feel like I can talk to you about anything."

"Anything?"

"Yeah," I chuckled.

"So, let me ask you this, why were you really at the hospital that day?"

That question threw me for a loop. I knew exactly why I was there, but I didn't expect her to question the explanation that I'd given her.

"What you mean by that?"

"Just curious. I didn't get the impression that you were there to check on him. I mean, I'm not judging your situation, but it's been on my mind since that day."

"I mean, I was there to check on my boy, that's it," I lied.

She just stared at me. I knew she didn't believe me, but why?

"You don't believe that," I asked.

"No. Like I said, I'm not here to judge but something tells me that you weren't there to check on him. I think you were there to finish the job."

"What? Nah, ma, you got it twisted. That's my homeboy."

"Okay, Marcus, let's change the subject," she said, rolling her eyes and focusing on the movie again.

"I really wanna know why you don't believe me."

"By your home, car, clothes and money, I know you don't do shit that's legal. I know you sell drugs. I'm not stupid. I grew up around it, my brothers do it, so I know a drug dealer when I see one. In the game, a nigga getting robbed and shot is a liability."

Her revelation shocked the hell outta me. She always seemed so innocent, like she had no idea of what I did. But this made me raise my eyebrow at her, in a good way, though. It kinda turned me on. I just hoped that by her having brothers in the game that she knew the rules. I didn't want to divulge personal information to her and she ended up getting me indicted. I decided I was gonna keep quiet about it and feel her out more.

"Mind ya business, ma," I told her.

I didn't want her sticking her button-nose where it didn't belong and end up on my hitlist. I had to feel her out more to see if she could be trusted. Even though Ava was a cheatin' hoe, she knew everything I did and never said a word. Some women could be trusted. I just had to figure out if Tiffany was one.

CHASE

Isabella had disappeared again. Just when I thought we were making progress, I'd call her and she wouldn't answer for days. I was trying my best to deal with it, but she was doing an awesome job at pushing me away. Like, what was the point of her doin' all this? One minute she all in my face, on my dick, then the next she's blocking my number and living her best life? What type of psycho can even do some shit like that?

That's a dumb question but still. I can only take so much. I'm still the same nigga that'll cheat on a bitch in a heartbeat and Isabella was trying hard to bring that nigga outta me. I sat there for a moment, thinking about how I could get back at Isabella and even the playing field a little. My mind was drawing a blank. A nigga had changed so much that he ain't even know how to plot revenge no more.

I figured it would come to me as I packed my bags and headed to the airport. I was going to Cali to meet up with my old team to discuss some work. Their connect had been indicted and the work was dryin' up severely.

Once I touched down, I went to Ronnie's crib. Yep, Kalani's brother. I knew it was a ninety-nine percent chance that I'd run into her when I came here, but I didn't care. If something happened between us, I would just blame it on Isabella ghosting me once again. I was for real, tired of that shit. She had no reason to still be doin' me like that yet, she was, every other fuckin' week.

"I was let in by none other than Ronnie. I hadn't seen him in over a year.

"Good to see you, nigga. Yo shit done grew out," I remarked, referring to his locs.

"Same here. And yeah dog, they gettin' there. This bitch I be smashin' put me on to this Loc Remedy Oil by this fine-ass girl named Ariel Waters. Her shit is the best," he replied.

"I see, my G. She must got some good shit cuz you usin' the whole government. But I remember when you could barely put them shits in a ponytail. Now you finna be rockin' a man bun in no time," I laughed.

"Nigga, you wylin'," he laughed back,

I followed him down the long hallway of his mini-mansion and to the living room, and there she was. Sitting Indian-style on the couch with her head in a book, Miss Kalani. She gave me a look of death when we finally locked eyes. She got up and quickly left the room when normally, she would've stayed. I wasn't tryna cause no friction, so I ignored it and sat down to discuss business with Ronnie.

"So, I'll just get straight to it. I'm stationed in Detroit right now and shit is crazy. I'm makin' more money than I ever have. I'd be willing to cut you in, cuz you ma dog, but I'd definitely have to run it by my partners, and they gon' wanna meet you. In the meantime, I can throw you a couple, on me, sound good?"

"Fuck yeah," he exclaimed.

"A'ight, book a flight to Detroit. And I got you."

"Cool."

We kicked it for a few, discussing the climate in Detroit, bitches, and money, then it was time for me to leave. When I got outside, Kalani was sitting on the porch, still reading.

"Can't speak?" I asked as I paused by the swingset she was sitting on.

"No," she snapped, closing her book and looking at me with that evil glare again.

"Why the fuck not?" I shot back, coming closer to her.

"Cuz you a piece of shit," she mumbled under her breath.

"Speak up, baby."

"You a hoe-ass nigga."

"Am I? Was I a hoe-ass nigga when I had you tellin' me you loved me?" The old me was resurfacing pretty quickly.

I just hated being made out to be the bad guy. Shit happens. I couldn't be responsible for every fuck up I made.

"You were. You the same nigga." I could see the hurt in her eyes, but I had a way to make that better.

"Can I make it up to you?"

"What? Hell no," she hissed, standing like she was ready to fight.

"Come here," I called.

"Nigga, no."

I came to her, wrapping my arms around her small waist. I couldn't stop myself from palming that ass while I spoke softly in her ear.

"You know you miss me. Wanna come chill wit' me tonight or you wanna keep playin' mad?" I made sure to rub my hard-ass meat on her thigh, just for a quick reminder. Bitches couldn't resist this big-ass dick.

"I don't wanna go nowhere wit' yo ass," she lied.

"Yeah, you do. Let me take you shopping. From what yo' brother told me, you ain't been in a while." I knew that was wrong, but I didn't give a fuck. I'd say anything to get what I wanted.

"No, that's not a good idea. I'm not about to let you play me again," she huffed, folding her arms.

"How is me taking you shopping, playin' you? Sis, get yo mind right and come on. I'll be in the car."

With that, I walked away and got back into my rental. She soon joined me, with a mean scowl and negative energy. It was okay, because soon she'd be happy again with my dick all up in her.

TRE

Niggas thought shit was sweet, but I was watching his every move. He was out again with the same chick from the restaurant, so I gathered that they were dating seriously. I bet that soft-ass fool was in love already. He always fell too easily. I had a plan, though. It took me some time but, I had it. It was grimy, but it was worth it.

Although I had my little revenge plot brewing, I still wanted to make my presence known. This nigga was not about to walk around like he owned the world. Not on my watch. I waited until they got inside and had been in there for quite some time. I knew he was tryna get some pussy, but later for that. I had a statement to make.

I picked the lock to the front door and crept inside. His crib was nice, I had to admit. He had decked it out, which meant he was comfortable here and would be staying for a while. I slid through the living room and continued looking around, searching for the perfect spot. Once I found the coffee table that looked like it was used frequently because of the ashes and tails of blunts, I sat the note down and crept back out. See, nothin' crazy, but he would certainly get the message.

The next day, I went and bought flowers again. This time, they were for someone else. I carried them with me inside the hospital where, you guessed it, Tiffany worked. I work fast, and I work smart. It also didn't hurt that I knew that Tiffany chick already. She was also Kalief's nurse when he got shot. If I knew one thing, I knew she had a knack for bad boys. She might have been an accomplished and degreed professional, but she was still a woman at the end of the day.

I went into the break room after figuring out her schedule. Yeah, I had watched her a few days. I had to get my ducks in a row if I was gonna successfully win this time.

"Nurse Tiffany," I called when I approached her.

She smiled back at me as I handed her the flowers.

"Who are these from?" she beamed, taking them from me and sitting them on the table.

"Me," I responded confidently.

"And you are?"

"I'm Joseph. I remember you being the nurse that took care of my homeboy when he got shot a couple months ago. I thought you did a wonderful job. It was also a pleasure to see such a beautiful face in a place like this," I flirted.

"Well, thank you. How is he by the way?"

"He was able to make a full recovery, thanks to you."

"Well, that is wonderful. I was really worried about his condition. I'm so happy to know he's doing better. This just made my day."

"You could make my day by letting me take you out," I suggested with my sly smile.

"Aww, I would, but I'm seeing someone."

"It's a harmless date. I just want you to know you're appreciated for your hard work, that's all. Pleaseee?"

"I guess one date couldn't hurt."

That was easy, but I knew it would be. Very few women could resist my charm. Sad to say but I was about to fuck my brother over again. Only this time, he deserved it. My phone started ringing and it was my brother, Chase.

"What's up?"

"Shit man, just checkin' in wit' you," he said.

"Everything good on my end. What about you?"

"I'm sweet, but I got something I need to talk to you about when I get back to Detroit tomorrow."

"A'ight, just hit me wit' a time and place."

"I got you."

After we hung up, I texted him a reminder for Kalief's baby shower next Saturday. I didn't want him to miss none of the festivities being that he was new to my crew. He knew everybody already, but it was a business-only atmosphere aside from the club opening. If everybody that was invited actually attended, it was gonna be a night to remember.

RICO

Time was winding down for my slut of a wife and her little boyfriend's love affair. I was sick of the lyin' and sneaking around she was doing. When she finally came home, I was not happy. I wanted to choke the fuck out her, but I remembered what happened that last time I put my hands on one of them. I still got a few scars. The way she sauntered in like she hadn't been missing in action for weeks completely blew me.

"Where the fuck you been?" I spat angrily as she tried to run up the stairs to our bedroom.

"I was with my family, in Georgia," she replied, frowning immediately at my accusatory disposition.

"Is *that* right?"

"Yeah. Where do you *think* I've been?"

"Come on, love, we both know that already."

"Well, I wasn't. I haven't been, and I don't plan to be. I'm married now, remember?"

"So, that's what kinda mood you in?"

"What mood, Rico?"

"The type of mood where you wanna play in my damn face." She was pissin' me off with the constant lies.

Yeah, I know I fucked up, a lot, but at least I wasn't reckless. I never fucked her sister but the way she was playin' me made me really wish that I had.

"Whatever. Call Mercedes and ask her," she shot back and walked away.

I don't know what type of marriage this was, but it was never what I imagined for us. I always planned on marrying her, however, these circumstances couldn't have been predicted. I never thought my wife would enter our marriage cheating. Hell, I never thought my wife would cheat at all. At one point, Kia wouldn't even look at another nigga. Now, she wasn't only lookin', but she was fuckin' em too. I had a plan for that as well.

I had been angry for two whole weeks, pacing the floor until I burned a hole in it thinking about her and what she was up to. She had me out here like one of these insecure bitches in a relationship with a cheatin' ass nigga. My, how the tables have turned. I now felt everything that I had made her feel over the years. Whenever she came to me with an accusation and I walked off like she just did me, I now understood how it felt to be her.

I loved her so much that I was willing to forgive her but her fuckin' boyfriend had to go. That was the only way that we would have any chance at a happy marriage. I did this. I brought this on myself by pushing her to the point of no return. If I had been doing right all this time, this wouldn't even be an issue, but it was, and I had the perfect way of handling it.

9

HELLO, GOODBYE

SIMONE

The preparation for my baby shower had my head spinning. I had a planner, but I wanted everything to be perfect, so I was involved and stressed from start to finish. It was lavish as hell, but that was expected for baby Kalief. My pregnancy was an easy one, especially since Kalief was there with me every step of the way. It was such a relief. The last time I was pregnant, it ended in a miscarriage from me being so stressed all the time.

I was frightened when I found out I was pregnant again. There was so much trauma when I was carrying my last baby. This is part of the reason I was so happy to have Kalief. He was nothing like Jerrod, the last guy I was pregnant by. I always wanted a baby and I was so happy that I had gotten pregnant by the right man this time. It was no way I should've miscarried because of duress. That nigga made my life a living hell.

The moment I found out I was pregnant by Jerrod, everything went downhill. He acted happy, but I could tell he wasn't. He started to stay out late, avoid me, miss doctor's appointments, the whole nine. I felt and looked stupid. He would start these crazy ass arguments and accuse me of cheating. He even wanted a paternity test because suddenly, I was cheating the whole time and couldn't be trusted. I mean, this guy did everything in his power to make me miserable. I remember it like it was yesterday.

I had already been put on bedrest at just four months. This dude literally threw fits every day because I wasn't well enough to cook for him. He was so selfish it made me sick, literally. He would constantly throw other women in my face, talking about what they were willing to do to have him. I was beyond angry and hurt. I was furious. Me arguing, yelling and fighting eventually made me lose the baby and Jerrod went with it. His ass "mysteriously" came up dead a few weeks after my miscarriage.

Remembering all of this made me so happy for my future. I finally had a good man after all the trauma I had suffered in my past. He was loving, attentive and everything I needed. We were great friends to begin with, so that foundation made our relationship that much better. Just thinking about him and the child growing inside of me made me smile. His daughter even loved me. Wish I could say the same about his spiteful baby mama, Kema, but fuck her. Anyone who tried their hardest to make a man like Kalief suffer, could rot in hell.

I took my time getting ready for my big day. You would've thought I was getting married the way my hair and makeup team was assembled. They were all dressed in blinged-out t-shirts with my name on them. We were also doing a big reveal of the baby's sex, so the venue was decorated both blue and pink with these huge, silver question-mark balloons. Everything met my requirements down to the food and I couldn't thank my event planner enough. She almost lost her mind twice dealing with me, but she got the job done.

"Thank you again, Lela, for all your hard work," I exclaimed, pulling her into a hug.

"I knew you wanted this to be perfect and I definitely brought that vision to life," she stated, tooting her own horn.

She deserved it. I had never seen a more perfect venue. Hell, I spent over twenty-five grand for it so I didn't expect anything less. After I was finished being pampered like the queen I was, it was finally time. My white, flowy dress was custom-made to fit my protruding belly and it even had the nerve to accent my curves. I was more than ready to show off my bump and wow my friends with this extravagant display I put on for baby Kalief.

JASMINE

The big day was here. I was running myself ragged because I'd waited until the last minute to prepare for Simone's shower. I made it pop though in a tan, backless knee-length dress with strappy stilettos and my signature gold clutch. I knew this was gonna be elegant because Simone wouldn't have had it any other way. She was extra just like everyone we ran with and I didn't expect anything less. I was honestly stunned by how well her venue was decorated. The colors jumped out at you. The centerpieces, which were bouquets of pink and blue artificial silk roses, looked real.

I sashayed in and found Kia who had come alone. I walked up to her smiling and pulled her into a hug.

"Where's Rico?" I asked.

"I don't know. I haven't seen him for a few days, but I know he wouldn't miss this for the world. He says he's the one responsible for knowing that Simone was even pregnant," Kia explained.

"So, what's up with you and Dro?"

"I haven't spoken to him either. Since I got back from visiting my fake-ass family in Georgia, I haven't seen or heard from him. I'm okay with it though because Rico had been giving me hell those couple days before he disappeared," Kia complained.

"Yeah, that side-nigga life can get stressful, can't it?"

"Oh, shut the hell up. As if yo' faithful ass would know."

"Don't do me. You don't know what type of life I've been living. Matter-of fact, I'll show you."

I had a trick up my sleeve. I decided to get a little messy and invite one of my high school friends to the baby shower as my date. Now, we hadn't slept together or anything, but I knew he always had a crush on me. His name was Cody and he had turned out to be fine as hell and a successful business owner. Back in the day he was a bad ass, knuckleheaded nignog known for fighting, stealing and everything else, but for some reason he was always nice to me. He would steal snacks from the store and always managed to bring me some chips, juice, and a honey bun. I never knew his snot-nose ass would turn out to be such an upstanding citizen. Not to mention, this damn fine. Cody obviously didn't have the best parents because he was always dirty, never had a haircut and barely had school clothes. Now he was sugar sharp, tall, had even brown skin, straight teeth, and reeked of money.

A smile crept onto Kia's face as he swaggered in, dressed to the nines in his tailored suit and shiny dress shoes. He was crispy as hell down to the fade and perfectly-trimmed goatee.

"You lookin' real nice, Jazzy," he commented after pulling me in for a hug.

"Thanks. You did that," I said, referring to his ensemble.

"This light," he said humbly.

"Cody, meet my best friend, Kia, the one I told you about," I said, introducing them.

"This the crazy one," he joked and we all laughed.

"Yes, it's me." She proudly came forward and shook his hand.

"I'm playin'. I've heard nothing but good things about you."

"Oh, I know. It's nothing but good things to be said. Now tell me, what type of crazy are you to be dealing with Jas and got the nerve to be smiling too?" Kia joked.

"Aye, you aint neva lied," he joined in with her like that shit was funny.

"Don't get beat up at this nice event," I warned the both of them.

Our little fun was soon interrupted by Rico walking toward us with this sly grin on his face.

"What's up, wife," he said to Kia but was more so letting Cody know she was married.

"What's up? How nice of you to show your face after your little disappearing act," she shot back.

Since I still wasn't talking to Rico, I didn't bother introducing him to Cody. He could kiss my ass. I stood there grimacing the whole time he was smiling in Kia's face like a fuckin' idiot. If I knew Rico, he had done something. I didn't know what exactly, but he did some shit during that three days he was gone.

"What's up man, I'm Cody, Jas' date," I heard Cody saying to Rico.

"I'm Rico. Jas' date, huh? Be careful, bruh," he laughed, tapping his shoulder. "She dangerous." Then he walked off toward Kalief who was coming in from another entrance.

"What he mean by that?" Cody questioned when Rico walked off.

"I'll fuck ya life up," I laughed. "But shit, I don't know. Maybe cuz I stomped his ass in a pair of timbs before." I shrugged.

"You what?"

"You heard me. It's a long story. I'll tell you later if you survive this," I chuckled, grabbing his hand and leading him toward Kalief and Simone.

Kia and I both greeted Kalief with warm hugs and congratulations. But it wasn't as warm when we got to Simone. I tried to fake it, we both did, but we couldn't. We were not happy with how Simone had been distancing herself and I'm sure she could tell by our embrace.

"How far along," I asked nonchalantly.

"I'm due next week," she smiled, rubbing her swollen belly.

"Damn, wish we could've been there," I sighed. I hoped she could feel how disappointed I was.

"I'm sorry y'all." She was near tears, so I decided not to ruin her moment and just hugged her.

Kalief smiled at us and sighed a sigh of relief. He knew just how serious shit could get between us when it came to our friendship.

TRE

I still hadn't heard from Jas. It had been almost three weeks. I was pissed that she hadn't even texted me or bothered unblocking my number. I went back and forth in my mind about if what I was about to do was the right thing. Deep down, I truly wanted to be with her. She was my fuckin' heart, but the way she was doin' me? I couldn't stand for that shit at all. She was deliberately playin' in my face. One minute she was all over me and the next I couldn't even call her phone without getting the voicemail.

During the last three weeks, I had been spending hella time with Tiffany. She was a cool chick and all, but she wasn't Jas. Did I want to be up under her as much as I was, no, but Jasmine left me no choice. See, at first, I was just gonna let Marcus catch me and Tiffany on a date, but since I was being played like a damn fool by my own girl, I decided platonic dating wasn't enough. So, I started fuckin' that bitch. Pussy was crazy, I ain't gon' lie. Her freak ass even let me tape her slobbin' all on this dick. She said I turned her out but nah, her ass was already out.

That shit was too easy. I was enjoying myself with her too. However, I couldn't stop thinkin' about Jas and how fucked up I was being right now. That shit had me depressed. I knew I was possibly gonna lose her forever, but my lust for revenge on both her and my brother was eating me alive. It wouldn't allow me to stop. Every time I thought about being locked up because of my brother or being locked out of Jas' life, I ended up knee-deep in Tiffany's wet-ass pussy.

In my honest defense, I tried to break it off with her a few times. I told her we shouldn't be doin' this, but that shit seemed to turn her on even more. Who would've thought this prissy-ass nurse would be such a nasty slut. You know I got a thing for sluts. She would ignore my texts about leaving her alone and be at my door in a trench coat with nothing under it thirty-minutes later. I couldn't say no to that shit if I tried.

Needless to say, I was now about to put the final nail in the coffin by bringing her as my date to Kalief and Simone's baby shower. Now, I did inform her that my most recent flame was gonna be here, to which she just smiled and waved me off. She was the sneaky type, so I had to watch her. Just knowing how she was behind closed doors and that we shared this dirty little secret, satisfied me in the weirdest ways.

It was showtime though and I was dressed to kill in a gray tailored suit with the matching kicks. Tiffany wore a black, ankle-length dress that snugly fit her wide hips and ass. She was built like Jessica Dime from Love and Hip-Hop. Yeah, so imagine all that ass in that tight dress. I was almost ready to be late fuckin' around wit' her.

We pulled up, valeted, and entered the venue. I held her small hand tightly, partly because I was nervous as fuck to see Jas. I felt like I was about to pass out from guilt as I got closer and closer to where they were all standing. Then I saw something that immediately took the breath out my ass. She was all hugged up with some tall-ass casket-sharp nigga. What the fuck was this?

I put some pep in my step with Tiffany barely able to keep up. I had to see what the hell was goin' on here. He was kissing her cheek and they looked like a happy couple. The fuckin' nerve.

"What's up man? Congratulations you two," I said to both Kalief and Simone.

I could hardly take my eyes off Jas to even properly acknowledge them.

"Thanks, bro. Who's your date?" Kalief asked snapping me out of my angry thoughts.

"Oh, my bad, this is Tiffany. The nurse that took care of you when you got hit."

"Oh, nice. It's nice to see you again," he told her, then gave her a hug.

Her and Simone started a side conversation and that was my cue to check the shit outta Jas. I walked a few steps over to where Jas, her li'l date, Kia, and Rico were standing. Jas was so up his ass, she hardly noticed I was there. When she did give me her attention, I caught the smirk that was on her face. That shit burned me up.

"What's up, Jas. This yo new man?"

"Cody, this is Tre, Tre this is Cody," she said smugly.

I was trying my best to conceal my jealousy, so I shook the nigga's hand then called Tiffany over to exact some revenge.

"This is Tiffany, *my* lovely date. Tiff meet Jas, her date, Kia and her husband Rico."

She spoke to everyone then walked off to use the ladies room. That gave me some time to better assess the situation.

"So, y'all in a relationship," I asked Cody.

"Nah, we just high school friends. Hadn't seen her in years."

"Tre, stay the fuck outta my business, though," she butted in as expected.

"No disrespect, baby, I was just askin' a question. I wanted to know who'd be taking my place from now on, that's all."

"You never had a place," she spat and pulled Cody off to the bar.

To make matters worse, I looked up and none other than the devil herself was making her way through the crowd, likely lookin' for Jas. Isabella shot me the dirtiest look as she switched past me in her cream-colored, tight-ass dress. That body was still amazing. When she didn't see her, she backed up and stood in front of me 'til I looked her way.

"Where's my cousin?" she asked with a snappy tone.

"Fuck that bitch," I snapped and walked off.

ISABELLA

I knew by the response that Tre gave me when I asked about Jas that she had obviously taken my advice. I told her she should show up here with a fine-ass date after pulling another one of her stunts on Tre. I finally found her and the guy she was with was indeed fine. My lips curled into a smile as I walked up to greet her and her beau.

"Good work, bitch," I whispered. "You got that nigga big mad."

"Let's go to the bathroom, I need to vent. Babe, I'll be right back, I have to use the restroom," she explained to her date. "Oh, by the way, this is my cousin Isabella, Izzy this is Cody."

"The one you used to tell me about when we were younger?"

"Yes, now come one," she snapped, dragging me to the bathroom.

"What's the tea, cuz you anxious as fuck," I whined when we were out of sight,

"Bitch, he brought some big-booty hoe here with him. I told you this was a bad idea."

"How? If you didn't bring Cody, you would've been the one embarrassed. That nigga is *pissed,* Jasmine. When I asked where you were he said, "fuck that bitch" and walked off. You win!"

"But I don't feel like I won. He didn't know I was bringing Cody, so he meant this shit. He was really tryna hurt me."

"Hurt people, hurt people. Jas, who are you? You actin' like some weak-ass bitch right now. That nigga is mad. He tried to bring this bitch here to make you jealous and you not. But he's still mad. What the fuck don't you understand?"

"You right. I'm just frustrated."

"You need some dick. Let's go get you drunk and un-frustrated and I know you giving Cody some pussy tonight, cuz I can feel that lustful demon on you right now," I joked.

By the way she burst into a fit of laughter, I was right.

"Mind ya business lady," she warned.

"Yeah, whatever, just tell me how that dick was tomorrow."

With that, we exited the bathroom and went straight to the bar. Kalief and Simone were on the mic talking about their relationship and how happy they were to be bringing a baby into the world. It made me sad because I didn't get to have a huge celebration when I was pregnant. I was in and out of the hospital, on bedrest, and sick from heartache because my baby daddy almost killed me.

I was getting all choked up as they spoke, so I ordered us a bottle of Hennessy at the bar and tossed back several shots to even out my sudden change of mood. After a while, I was getting nice and toasted. I was so toasted that I hadn't even noticed that my baby daddy was here and had a bitch on his arm. The same bitch he was at the hotel with. I almost lost my whole mind. My eyes followed them as they roamed the crowd speaking to guests until they got to Kalief and Tre. Jas saw what I saw, and her eyes bucked.

"I hate to ruin your girl's baby shower but somebody gon' die tonight," I murmured.

"Chill cousin, didn't you tell me that I had it under control? Hurt people, hurt people and all that shit," Jas rebutted.

"Don't fuckin' play wit' me right now," I threatened. My tone was serious as fuck.

"Follow yo' own advice then bitch," she spat and walked off.

Then she backpedaled and whispered in my ear, "You fuck up my brother's baby shower over yo trife-ass baby daddy, and I swear I'll fuck *you* up."

I took her warning into consideration as my eyes still burned a hole through the back of Chase's stupid-ass head. I was livid. Then I saw Tre making a beeline toward me, not giving me a chance to prepare for the bullshit he was about to spit to me.

"You picked the wrong brother. Marcus would never do that to you," he chuckled, then walked off.

I was so angry and embarrassed, I could've cried. That bitch was all draped across his arm like she was some important chick. She wasn't shit but another one of his hoes and a pastime. She didn't even know she was being used. Poor thing. I decided to chill for the moment because the way my temper and nostrils were flaring, this beautiful venue would be up in flames.

KALIEF

Simone might not have noticed everything that had transpired, but I did. The tension in the room was thicker than Tre's date. Last time I checked, Tre and Jas were serious, now they had both shown up with different people. I didn't know Isabella or Chase too well, but last I checked, they were also an item. By the way she shot daggers at him and his date, I knew some shit was bound to pop off at any minute.

I didn't want any drama at this celebration. I didn't think there would be any but made niggas always had security wherever they went. I would hate for one of my friends to have to get carried out, but that was the way it was lookin'.

Simone's hostess for the big day got on the mic and announced that we were about to do the big reveal. She didn't tell me the sex of the baby because she wanted it to be a surprise. I agreed. I loved surprises. Well, good ones anyway. I wanted a boy so bad that I was on pins and needles waiting for this exact moment.

A video started to play on the projector that highlighted some of the moments we had shared in our relationship. Even old pictures when we were still just friends. Even those photos showed the chemistry she and I shared. It was evident that one day, we'd be together.

After the video finished, this display of flickering pink and blue lights started to flash around us. My daughter, Jayla held my hand as she prepared to know if she would be getting a brother or sister. She too wanted a brother so we both had been praying every night that Simone was having a boy. I was nervous as shit when the lights stopped. They stopped on pink, though. I sighed inwardly but honestly, a baby with Simone made me happy regardless of sex. We would just keep trying until we got a boy.

Then the ceiling opened, and all these blue balloons fell to the floor. They all read "It's a Boy." I liked to had cried. Well, I did a little. I grabbed and hugged Jayla and Simone so tight. Jayla and I were ecstatic because our prayers had been answered. Everyone roared with congratulations and crowded around us for hugs and pictures of the big reveal.

After that dissipated, there was still plenty of food for the guests, so we played a few games, and everyone continued drinking. In the midst of it all, one special guest came in that I knew security was gonna have to escort out soon. It was Marcus. That was my nigga and he'd never done anything to me, but I knew the beef he had with Tre was dangerous. I looked around for Tre who was oblivious to the fact that his brother and archnemesis was even here.

"What's up, bro. Sorry I'm so late. I got tied up, but congratulations to you and your lovely lady on the baby boy, I see," he smiled.

"Yeah man, I almost cried."

"I know, bro. That's what them beautiful babies do to you."

We rapped for a minute then he walked off to get some food and a drink from the bar. Then he spotted his brother and all hell broke loose. I crept closer to make sure he ain't have a weapon. What I heard next threw me for a loop.

"You here wit my bitch?"

This nigga, Tre had done it again. I mean, I guess it was revenge for Marcus framing him for murder, but he framed him cuz he found out Tre had fucked his baby mama. I shook my head at it all. The two brothers lunged at each other and a brawl ensued. People started screaming, some were tryna break it up, but these two were like the Hulk and Iron Man goin' at it. They were crashing all over the place, knocking over tables and chairs as guests scrambled to avoid the collision.

Then I saw security rushing toward them in the nick of time. They had successfully pulled the brothers apart and were escorting them toward the door when I heard a familiar scream. It was Simone. I rushed over only to find her standing in a puddle. Her water had broken. At that moment, I didn't give a fuck what was goin' on. Everybody had to get the fuck out the way.

"Y'all move, my baby water broke!" I yelled so loud the room shook.

Security rushed to clear a path as I walked Simone to the front door. Everyone, including Tre and Marcus stepped to the side and allowed us to get by. When we approached the door, suddenly, a dark figure came from out of nowhere and slashed Simone across the face. She screamed loudly as blood leaked from her cheek.

"What the fuck!" I immediately dove into action, chasing after the person, but that muhfucka was fast. I lost them when they bent the corner.

I rushed back to Simone to assess the damage. It wasn't as bad as I thought, but she was definitely gonna need stitches. Someone had already called an ambulance and my guests had grabbed the emergency kit and started to tend to her facial wound.

"I can't believe this shit!" Simone was crying like a baby as she sat there with blood soaking her gown.

I was ready to kill only I had no idea who would do some shit like this. Luckily, there were surveillance cameras outside of the venue. My baby had gone into labor and got stabbed on her way out the door on her big day. Somebody was gonna pay for this shit.

10
_____

THE RECOVERY

JASMINE

After the baby shower fiasco, I sat my ass still for a while. I was so rattled up by everything that transpired that night that I was literally in tears and shaking like a leaf. My best friend got her face slashed at her own fuckin' celebration. Like, who the fuck would be crazy enough to do that? What possible enemies did she have? Were they even after her? All these questions swirled in my mind on the drive to Beaumont to see her.

She had successfully birthed her baby boy, Kalief Jr., and was in recovery with stitches in her face and pussy because he split her so bad. Kalief got a big-ass head so I knew that baby boy was gonna fuck her up. My boo, Simone was a warrior and I knew she would push through this like she did everything else.

KJ was still in the nursery waiting to be carted to his family in the hospital room. We told the nurses several times to bring him to us because we were all anxious as hell to see the beautiful chocolate drop. Everyone was there, including Tre's disgusting, disrespectful ass. I partly blamed him for everything including Simone's stab wound. It was about the timing. If he hadn't been fighting, her water wouldn't have broken, and she wouldn't have been at the door at that moment to get her face sliced.

I was fuming in the waiting room having to look at his face and be in his presence. He had a look of worry and regret as he kept staring at me like I was really gonna acknowledge he existed right now. I felt sick. He literally made me wanna puke. I kept an evil glare plastered on my face as I rocked back forth trying to calm myself. Just when I was about to pop, Kalief came and announced the baby was on his way for us to see. Kia was so excited that she almost screamed when Kalief said it was time.

We were already washed and had our scrubs on. We went in two at a time with Kia and I being buddies to smile and coo at the precious little baby boy that was now our nephew. I couldn't wait to spoil him.

Kalief couldn't stop holding him and I swore I saw that nigga drop a few tears. He had every reason. He had helped to create this perfect little soul that looked exactly like him. After a while, he wanted to go check on Simone and send the baby back to the nursery, so we all said our goodbyes and left him alone.

On the way out, Tre followed me to my car and I tried my damndest to get in before he was close enough to stop me. I didn't make it before he snatched me away from the door and planted this disgusting kiss all over my mouth. I fought to get away then spit on the ground next to his feet.

"Why you keep fuckin' playin' me, man!?" Tre yelled so loud that everyone looked directly at us. I was so embarrassed.

"Tre, get the fuck away from me," I said in almost a whisper as I tried to get in my car again.

He wasn't havin' it. He grabbed me again, this time in a bear hug and pleaded with me to talk to him.

"I have nothing to say."

"Yes, you do. Tell me you hate me or something, just talk to me."

"You're not even worth the energy, now move. Them white people finna call the police," I warned.

He eased up and I got in my car and buckled up. I watched him jog to his car and of course, he followed me. I went home because I was supposed to go to Cody's to get my pussy rearranged, but with

Tre on my ass, that wasn't a good idea. I had given him a call to cancel, threw the towel in, and pulled up to my crib. I huffed loudly as I got out and saw Tre coming toward me. He wasn't gonna give up.

I let myself in and tried in vain to close the door in his face. He pushed past me, giving me a glare that asserted his dominance. I wanted him to leave but it wasn't happening. He was already inside.

"Jasmine, can we please just talk?"

"Talk about what? You got a new bitch that's obviously your brother's girl, *again*. You ain't shit and certainly not the type of nigga I need to be around. That nigga gon' fuck around and kill yo' ass and I'm not getting caught in the crossfire," I spat, folding my arms across my chest.

"Baby, please, I'm under a lot of stress. I'm fully aware I fucked up this time. That's why I'm here. You just keep on tryna hurt me. Every other day I'm on the block list. Every time I think we getting better, you disappear again and show me that we not. I can't take that shit no more, Jas," he said dropping to his knees and hugging my waist.

"Tre, get up. Get yo' stupid ass up."

"Babyyyy, pleaseeee. I can't be without you."

This nigga was actually cryin'. I tried hard not to laugh.

"Get up! Stop this. I don't wanna hear it. You been fuckin' that bitch, go cry to her," I said angrily.

"And you been fuckin' that nigga, right? Haven't you?! Don't fuckin' lie to me man," he growled.

He was so close to my face and the nigga was cryin'. I knew that when niggas got this emotional to be careful. They weren't stable.

"Don't ask me anything."

"Huh!? You let that nigga have *my* pussy?"

"You let that bitch have my dick," I shot back to even the score.

That didn't work. He grabbed my neck and started choking me.

"Tre, stop!"

"You fucked that nigga? Huh?"

He picked me up and put me on the table in my dining room, still holding my neck. He wasn't choking me hard, but I felt the anger coursing through his veins.

"Answer me! Answer my fuckin' question," he barked, releasing his grip on my neck and making me look at him.

I was so scared. I started to cry.

"Leave me alone, pleaseeee," I whined.

"He fuck you better than me? Just answer that and I swear I'll leave you alone."

"Does she fuck you better than me?" I shot back.

"Fuck no! Don't nobody fuck me like you. This my pussy now come here!"

He snatched me off the table and backed me down the hallway to my room. Bitch, I couldn't lie, I was turned on. I don't even know why. This nigga was crazy as shit but that just made my pussy throb even more. He ripped off my shirt and bra, stuffing my nipple in his mouth while gently massaging the other. I took my own leggings off cuz that's how bad I wanted that dick.

"I fuckin' hate you, dog, I swear," I huffed as he pinned my naked body against the wall.

"I feel the same. I literally wish I could end yo life right now."

Then he snatched me up and threw me on the bed. He got on his knees and buried his face in my twat. When I say this nigga made me see stars. He fingered me and sucked my clit simultaneously 'til tears poured out of my eyes. All I could hear was him moaning, smacking and slurping on my shit like it was Thanksgiving dinner.

"Mmm, my pussy taste so good," he moaned as he continued to suck the soul outta me.

Then he went down further and stuck his tongue in my ass. I liked to had lost my mind. My moans got louder and louder and he switched between my pussy and ass with his thick tongue.

"He suck that pussy better than me, bitch?" Tre growled from beneath me, where he belonged.

"Nooooo! I swear to Goddd," I cried as he devoured me.

Once he was satisfied, he fully disrobed and made me get on my knees. The look of lust he had while staring at my mouth sent chills through my pussy. He shoved his whole dick down my throat, causing me to gag violently. After catching my breath, I let him fuck my mouth and talk shit to me all he wanted. He called me every name in the book while his face twisted up in pleasure. His moans were so loud and sexy that I had no choice but to rub my pussy 'til I came. What type of bitch orgasms off giving head? This one.

"Daddy made you cum by fuckin' that pretty mouth, huh?"

"Yeahhh," I panted, trying to recover.

I was scared to even get the dick. That nigga was in beast mode. He punished this pussy so good that I thought I would pass out. I nutted on that dick so many times my pussy pulsated for nearly an hour after we finished. I just couldn't stop fuckin' him.

KIA

Shit had been crazy since the baby shower. I had been checking on Simone every single day. I couldn't imagine what she felt like after all that had happened. It was supposed to be one of the happiest moments of her life, but she ended up going into labor and getting stabbed. She wasn't letting it get to her, though. She was too busy smiling at KJ and loving him like I knew she would. Even through her stitches and bandages, her beauty seemed to be magnified from giving birth. The glow she had because of her child was apparent.

After visiting her and the baby for a few hours, I decided to go home. I took the scenic route because I had a lot on my mind. By a lot, I meant Dro. I hadn't heard from him in a while and I was past pissed; I was worried. It wasn't like him not to call or text me. It had been weeks since I heard from him. Was he done with me and wasn't gonna officially break it off? Had he found a new bitch to replace me with? I was irreplaceable, so I shoved that thought out of my mind.

Things with Rico had gone back to normal. He was smiling every day. He was bringing me gifts and being sweet. There was no more mention of me cheating and he didn't accuse me of sneaking around anymore. I don't know what caused the sudden change and although it's what I wanted, something seemed fishy.

I would be keeping an eye on Rico every day. He was up to no good. Maybe he got Dro to leave me alone for good. I didn't know but I damn sure was gonna find out. I called Dro's phone several times and got the voicemail. I knew with his line of work that he could be on a business trip, but he hadn't hit me up at all. This wasn't like him and I was starting to get worried.

In the meantime, I would keep my ear to the streets to try to find out what was going on with my man and his mysterious absence. I just prayed, for Rico's sake, that he didn't have anything to do with his disappearance. I was trying to keep myself busy and my mind off Dro, so I called Jas to see if she could help. Plus, I needed the tea.

"I'm outside and I'm not comin' in if yo' psycho-ass husband is here," she huffed on the other end of my phone.

I didn't have time for her drama, so I kindly slipped on my gym shoes and joined her in the car.

"So, what's the tea bitch?" I asked before I could even properly seatbelt myself.

"I made a mistake and fucked Tre," she said in barely a whisper.

"Speak up!"

"I fucked Tre, damn."

"Okay, what's wrong with that?"

"After he brought that bitch in my face? He ruined Simone's baby shower. He's trash, and I still couldn't control myself."

"You in love, what do you expect?

"I expect to be able to drop a nigga with no warning and that be it. But I should've learned from Monty that it doesn't happen that easy, especially not with this good pussy," she laughed.

"You a whole mess. But peep this, why the fuck haven't I heard from Damien in weeks? Rico been around the house acting like he loves me so much. He's been happy, smiling, singing and shit like he won the Powerball or something. And I find it odd that Dro would just stop calling me like that. I mean, we hadn't had any arguments or nothing. Even if we did that would be more reason for him to blow my phone up."

"Well, I'll ask around and see if anyone heard from him. That don't seem right to me either," she assessed.

Lighting up a blunt she had already rolled, she hit it a few times at the stoplight and passed it to me. We continued driving until we reached her house. Stepping inside, I noticed she had cooked a big-ass meal and had snacks and movies.

"Oh, this a sleepover," I joked.

"Yes, because I need my bestie and we can go visit Simone tomorrow without them funky-ass niggas around. I'm sick of lookin' at them."

"I heard that. KJ is so adorable, isn't he?"

"Girl, oh my God, I couldn't stop staring at him. Makes me wanna get off birth control and let a nigga shoot my club up," Jas laughed.

"I swear! But later for that." I knew a baby with Rico would be pure hell, especially with the way he acted, period.

He may have been cool now but he would really think he ran shit if he got me pregnant.

～

We were in the hospital with Simone and the baby. She was recovering just fine, and we were both pleased to know she was feeling better.

"I can't wait to get home to my own bed, but I've been good. Pushing though as always," Simone said, trying to reposition herself while breastfeeding KJ.

"And I wanna get everybody together, with the exception of one person and do a little dinner for Simone's birthday in a couple weeks," Kalief told us.

"Okay, can we be in charge of that? I mean, since we didn't get a hand in planning the baby shower," Jas said unhappily.

"Yes, I would love that," Simone smiled.

After we left, Jas looked up some spots where we could have a big, private dinner and we both agreed on the same place. It was this huge hall and we would get the event catered. As much as I loved planning events with Jas, I was sour as hell that Simone didn't let us plan her shower. But I put that behind me in order to mend our friendship. She had been through a lot this past year. We all had.

Jas and I went our separate ways and it was back to crazy-ass Rico for the next few days. He was still in his good mood and quite frankly, I didn't like it. I knew my man.

"Everything all right, wifey? You been seeming a little down lately."

"I'm good. You've been seeming a little too up for my liking lately."

"I'm just happy you're back. I fuckin' missed you. I don't know why you don't think I love you, but I do. You everything to me wit' yo fine ass." He kissed my cheek so lovingly.

"You layin' it on real thick I see." I loved his kisses. I leaned in so he could kiss me some more.

I already knew where this was going. Right between my legs. It felt like I hadn't been with Rico in forever. So, when he entered me, I gasped and held back moans. He made love to me so passionately that I wanted to forgive everything and just stay here with him forever. However, the next day, my whole life changed in the blink of an eye.

SIMONE

I was nervous as hell about doing another event after the last one I had ended the way it did. It was my birthday though, so I tried to push all of that to the back of my mind and enjoy this special occasion. Now, one good thing was, I snapped the fuck back just three weeks after having my son and I looked good. I had no stretch marks; my stomach only had a tiny pudge and everything else on me was bigger. These hips, ass and titties included.

Kalief couldn't keep his eyes off me as I oiled up and slipped on my dress for the evening. I could tell he was ready to get all up in this, but he couldn't and that was driving him crazy. The way he lustfully ogled my body made me smile inwardly. He was still very much attracted to me even after giving birth. That was a huge change in a woman's life and I had no idea how he'd react to it but seeing his eyes roam all over me gave my self-esteem a boost.

Once I was finished getting ready, we packed up KJ and sent him with my mom. I didn't want him around groups of people until I felt it was safe. We made it to the hall where my birthday dinner was being thrown. I couldn't wait to see what Jas and Kia had done as far as decorating because they did have a knack for detail. We all did. I knew it would be spectacular.

It was. Walking inside, there were balloons everywhere in my favorite colors, black and silver. There were pictures of me posted on the walls and a huge banner that said, "Happy Birthday, Simone." The tables had a picture of me on them as well. I guess these bitches thought that I was that much of a narcissist. I had to laugh cuz I was. They greeted me as I walked in and all the guests stood up and cheered as I made my entrance. I strutted like a fashion model up to the mic to thank everyone for coming.

As the night went on, we ate, drank and danced and all was right in the world. There was no drama. Everyone seemed to be with their right match tonight. Jas and Tre were together, Kia and Rico looked happy, and Isabella and Chase even sat together. I couldn't have asked for a better party.

Everyone started getting on the mic, spilling about our friendship and how much they loved me. I felt so good that I dropped a few tears. Then Kalief got up and asked me to join him. This was gonna be good. I loved when my baby talked about me to people. He was grateful to have me and had nothing but kind words. He went on and on about how he knew we were meant to be. I turned my head for one split second as someone handed me some water because I was getting choked up. When I turned around, this man was on one knee with a ring as big as the lump in my throat. Everyone went crazy with cheers. I just covered my face and cried like never before. I couldn't believe this.

"Will you marry me?" he asked after noticing that I wasn't even capable of talking.

I just fell into his arms, nodding my head "yes" and hugging him tightly. Then confetti started to fall and all I can say is, I was the happiest woman in the whole world. Everything was perfect that day and I wished I could've stayed in that moment forever. Luckily, there was a videographer and plenty of people snapping pictures.

I was on cloud nine every day after. When we got home, Kalief stressed to me that I needed to start planning the wedding ASAP. That was what made me know he was serious about me. Some men propose and then would be engaged for years to come. He was ready to walk down that aisle immediately. Life had its ups and downs but the good always outweighed the bad.

11

A WEDDING AND A FUNERAL

MARCUS

I almost killed Tiffany that night. I didn't though because she explained that Tre had brought her there because she had been Kalief's nurse while he recovered from his bullet wounds. I knew my brother didn't know we were dating and this time; it was merely a coincidence. After she pleaded for her life and told me she would never speak to him again, I allowed her to live.

She had been mad at me all week and she had every right. I didn't want her to be afraid of me, so I sat her down and told her everything that had transpired between he and I and the whole reason for our beef. She took it all in and didn't flinch as I hit her with some shit I knew she wasn't prepared for. I told her what I did for a living because I felt like I could trust her. If I couldn't, she would end up like everybody else that crossed me.

She had me open enough to divulge those details to her. I couldn't believe it my damn self. She was good for me and I wanted to keep her around. I had even brought her around my kids, so her ass was permanent until she fucked up. I knew eventually she'd forgive me for the mild torture I had put her through that night. She understood what I had been through with my brother and my women and she claimed that she would be different.

She had opened me up to a lot, and like I said before, her heart was big and her love for helping people won me over from the beginning. Things were definitely getting serious between us. I know I always moved fast, but this time, Tiffany was moving fast right along with me. I couldn't have asked for a better girl and I silently prayed that she stayed perfect, cuz I wouldn't hesitate to body her ass if she pulled any of the shit I had told her about.

I didn't think I would have to go that route because of the course of the next month, she was nothing but solid. We grew closer every day. It was crazy how quickly I had fallen for her. After she told me her background, I met her brothers. I had half-a-mind to partner up with them and ditch my brother's organization. At any moment, that nigga could pull the plug on me. I knew Chase wouldn't let that happen, but Tre had a knack for getting his way.

I had a lot to think about and a lot of things were unclear. One thing that was crystal though was the fact that I had finally found someone that cared about me, that I could relate to and, that hadn't fucked my brother even though she had been around him. I wanted to lock that down as quickly as possible.

KIA

I had been keeping my composure around Rico. He was obviously out of his mind. I didn't know what would happen if I confronted him about Dro, so I kept quiet. I wanted to kill his ass. When I found out that Dro was dead after hearing the report loud and clear from Jas, I wanted to die my damn self. It was too much for me to handle. I couldn't take knowing I would never see him again and I couldn't even pay my respects. It was no way in hell he would go almost two months without contacting me.

I took the advice of Jas and Isabella and went on a vacation with them for a while. They were always leaving out of the clear blue to get away from their sorry-ass niggas and I had one triflin'-ass piece of shit sharing a bed with me every night. He would smile in my face knowing the fucked-up shit he did behind my back. I knew I couldn't trust him anymore. If he did that to Dro, knowing how dangerous he was, he wouldn't hesitate to kill my ass too. That's the only reason I stayed quiet.

I couldn't fake my cool anymore, so I packed my bags and got the fuck out of dodge with the girls. This had become one of their rituals. They would put Tre and Chase on the block list and live their best lives out of the state or country, whatever way the wind blew.

We were on a plane to Havana, Cuba. I don't know what compelled them to go there, but I was prepared. During the five-hour flight, I slept to avoid crying. I knew if I stayed up, I would probably throw the whole vibe off. I thought sleeping would put me in a better mood. It didn't. As soon as we got into our hotel room, the waterworks began.

"I can't fuckin' believe he killed him," I wailed in Jas' lap.

"Kia, we don't know who did it."

"Yes, we do. We might not have solid proof, but that nigga did it."

"It's gonna be okay, boo. And I didn't tell you he died. My source didn't say he passed, they said he got shot up really bad."

"And what else?"

"Ant that it ain't lookin' good but—"

"Okay so, bitch have you seen him? Heard from him? No! He's dead, Jas." I was screaming and crying at the top of my lungs.

"Kia, calm down. I promise you will be good," Jas said, trying to console me.

"No, this is fucked up. Regardless of how y'all treat Tre and Chase, y'all love them. Y'all can go home to them whenever y'all feel. I gotta go home to a fuckin' murderer."

"Kia, they all murderers, boo," Jas said, and I almost laughed cuz that shit was funny.

"But you know what I mean. I don't care if I ended up choosing Rico over Dro, I didn't want him dead," I sobbed some more.

They tried their best to comfort me, but it was all in vain. I had nightmares the whole trip and I know I was a stick in the mud. I was sure they both understood what I was dealing with though because they always came to my rescue when I was having a fit. I missed him so much that I never thought I would recover.

CHASE

Shit still hadn't gone back to normal between Isabella and me. She still hadn't gotten over me bringing Kalani to Simone's baby shower. I knew it would take her some time because she never got over anything that fast. In the meantime, I was still seeing Kalani behind her back. She could keep playing her games. I was just gonna play them too.

She was still playing the blocking game as well, so guess what? I blocked her punk-ass too. I was focused on the woman who was focused on me. Kalani was nothing to break down. She was in love with me still, even after all the weak shit I did. I had feelings for her, somewhere in my heart, but to me, she let me get away with too much. Isabella would never. Still in all, I kept her around for my own comfort, knowing I was gonna dispose of her as soon as Izzy got her muthafuckin' mind right.

Right now, she was somewhere chillin' on a beach not thinkin' about my ass while I couldn't keep her off my mind. I wanted things to be right between us, but not at my own expense. I wasn't about to keep chasing her around like it wasn't bitches that would do anything to be with me. She had another thing coming if she thought I was that nigga. I loved her to death, but at this point she was making my life hard. She was fuckin' our family up all to get some revenge.

Both of us should've been at home with Lola. We shoulda been married by now, but no. Isabella just couldn't be tamed. I didn't wanna give up, but I was thinkin' it was needed in order for me not to do nothin' crazy. She was liable to make a nigga flip out for real and I couldn't have that. I was clueless as to how I could make this relationship work.

While Kalani and I fucked like it was no tomorrow, I had to shake my head at myself. She told me she was on birth control and we both ain't play about them papers, so we didn't use contraceptives. I don't know why, but my feelings resurfaced quickly after I came in her. Shit was weird as hell. I knew I needed to stay away from her because I was gonna lose at my own game. I couldn't get over her sweet personality. She was the girl that I knew I needed but Isabella was the one I really wanted.

However long we had, I was gonna make the most out of it. I really didn't wanna hurt Kalani, but I knew I would if Isabella decided we were gonna be together. Who knows what she would do at the end of the day, though? She was so wishy-washy, and that shit blew me. I would be MIA until she made up her mind and decided to come back. And her ass was still on the blocklist, so she would have to find a way to contact me if she wanted me.

RICO

"Aye, we need to talk, man to man," I said to Dro.

"Set it up," he responded, sounding agitated.

I knew he was probably tired of the back and forth over Kia, but hey, so was I.

I told him to meet me at the warehouse at nine the next day. I wasn't coming to talk, I was coming to kill. When I got there, I saw him standing against the brick wall. He was dressed in a hoodie and jeans. I could barely make out his face the way he was all covered up.

I didn't waste time. I had my gun cocked and let the bullets fly. It was over for him and my wife sneakin' around behind my back. His dead body crashed onto the pavement as he bled out from all the holes I filled him with. I took the fuck off after that. I knew he wouldn't make it if ten paramedics tried to resuscitate his ass.

I knew it would break Kia's heart if and when she found out, so I had been extra nice and sweet until the streets started talking. Her ass had dipped on me and I knew she was somewhere cryin' her eyes out over that nigga. I didn't give a fuck. If a nigga thought he was gon' steal my woman, he had another thing comin.' I had been with her for years and we were married now. She wasn't goin' nowhere.

I paced the floor as usual, calling her phone back-to-back. I hated not being able to get in touch with her. Shit had me stressed and worried. What if she called herself leaving me? I knew how them bitches got down. Jas had Tre out here finna lose patches of his hair fuckin' wit' her. I hated this shit. I needed a bitch I could control.

"Aye, Kia, I know you see me callin' you. At least let me know you all right," I said on her voicemail.

After trying her a few more times, I decided to give up for now. I had a meeting to get to. Chase wanted us to sit down with some nigga named Ronnie that needed some work and we had all agreed. I drove to the meeting, barely being able to concentrate because of Kia. I was scared to lose her, and she had every reason to leave my ass. It was no doubt in my mind that she had discovered that Dro was no longer with us.

I pulled up at the club where we had all of our important meetings, including our drug deals. By the line of luxury vehicles parked next to each other, I was the only one missing. I put a little pep in my step cuz I wasn't in the mood for nobody to be checking me about my time of arrival.

"What's up, fellas?" I spoke as I finally joined them.

"What up," Chase said. "A'ight, let's get started. This my boy, Ronnie, who I worked with out in Cali before I came here and set up shop with y'all. His plug got locked down and now he's lookin' for work. Since I trust him, I thought maybe he could join the team. He already had his payment for the first shipment if y'all will allow it."

We all had questions, that was protocol, but him coming with a reference like Chase, our minds were made up. We allowed him to join and everything went as planned. He picked up his shipment and went about his way.

After the meeting, we all sat around to have a little conversation about our women. Since they all ran together, this was the perfect time for us to gripe about their attitudes.

"I'm willing to bet all three of them somewhere huddled up laughing about all the bullshit they been doin'," Tre said.

"You know it. This shit is like a ritual for them. But see, while they on dumb shit, I been havin' some fun of my own. Bitches think shit sweet, you feel me," Chase replied.

"You already know. Kia got a rude awakening when she realizes her fuckin' boyfriend dead," I blurted out.

Nobody knew that but me and I didn't want anyone to know yet.

"Wait what? You did that shit?" Tre asked with a look of bewilderment.

"I ain't say I did it," I quickly tried to retract my statement.

Killing Dro was bad for business. It could and would start a war. I wasn't ready for that right now. Although I knew nothing could tie me to his murder, it wouldn't stop niggas from retaliating against me because I was the nigga who had issues with him.

"Nigga, yes you did. Do you know what you did?" Tre asked, sounding like he was scared.

"You soundin' real pussy right now."

"Nah, you soundin' real stupid right now. You don't do shit like this without a plan. You know how him and his crew get down and you choose to make a move like that? Over some pussy? Nigga, you crazy. We ain't survived the game all these years by doing shit off emotions. No matter who it was, weak or strong, we always had a plan."

Tre was right. I had fucked up big time.

"For right now, I didn't have shit to do wit' it and let's leave it at that." I didn't have time for a history lesson. I needed to get home and start developing a plan.

When I got there, shit was evident that somebody knew something. There was a note waiting for me in my mailbox. It simply read, "She's not coming home."

FUCK!

JASMINE

It was good to be back home after our trip. I wasn't looking forward to having Tre on my doorstep when I got back, but I didn't expect to feel so stupid when he wasn't. I had the nerve to be appalled. I had to laugh at myself for a moment. What the hell was wrong with me? I went out of my way to avoid him and still wanted him to be there when I got back. If I wasn't in love, I don't know what the hell to call this shit.

I went inside to unpack my clothes and my feelings. Next thing I knew I was getting drunk and calling him back to back because now, he had the nerve to be sending me to voicemail! I decided to hop my drunk ass in the car and head over to his place. I wasn't about to play games with his ass. I was mad as hell that he would do some shit like that when he was the one that fucked everything up in the first place.

I was speeding down the freeway and made my exit. I was swerving from lane to lane like a bat out of hell. I finally came to his street and darted right into the back of his car as it pulled out of the driveway. All I saw was black while tasting blood before I completely lost consciousness.

~

The next day I woke up in a hospital bed. I was attached to all these monitors and IVs. I was scared as shit. I looked up and saw Tre sitting there. He had worry written all over his face.

"Oh my God, baby, you're awake!" He quickly jumped up to kiss me and it hurt like hell when his mouth touched mine.

"What the fuck happened." I barely was able to get that out.

"All I know is I was pulling out of my driveway and you slammed into my car. I called the ambulance and they brought you here. Your blood/alcohol level was sky high. Why the fuck was you so drunk?"

"I was mad at you."

"Jas, what the fuck? Really? So, what were you coming to do, fight?"

"I don't know." I had started to cry.

I felt so bad about what I had done. I almost killed myself all because of my need for revenge. I wanted to hurt him so bad that I ended up hurting myself. I still partly didn't give a fuck. He deserved that shit and more. I just didn't need to be drunk and driving. My mixed emotions were getting the best of me. I felt so right being in his arms, the sex was spell-binding and I did love him, but part of me still felt like he didn't deserve me, and he still needed to be punished.

"Baby, just promise me you won't do no shit like that again. And please stop disappearing on me. I won't be able to take that shit after what happened just now."

He was right. If it wasn't his car I ran into, and I wound up here, everybody would've been worried sick. I just didn't know how to handle my emotions these days. Every time I felt overwhelmed by this constant love/hate struggle, I ran away. It was too much for me. I still had so much trauma to deal with at the hands of the men I loved, and I just couldn't take it at times. I felt like I was drowning. I felt stupid for still being in love with someone who wanted to kill me at a point.

"I know. I won't do it again."

"Jas, I swear to Godddd," he went on, but I interrupted him

"I said I won't now shut up."

After the nurse came in and told me that I only suffered some minor injuries, I was sent home the next day with a prescription for pain meds. Tre insisted on staying at my place to keep an eye on me. I did everything I could to convince him that I was fine, but he wasn't havin' it.

"I ain't payin' you no mind. You can barely walk. I'm movin' in until you're better and I can trust you to stop runnin' off. You need some in-house for a while anyway. We both do," he said like he ran shit.

I just huffed and puffed and rolled my eyes while I waited in the car for him to grab his things and temporarily invade my personal space. The few weeks that he was there were nothing short of amazing, though. He massaged me every single day, cooked for me, showered me, dressed me. He treated me like a damn patient in the nursing home, aside from fuckin' me crazy. I hated to say it, but I was getting used to this shit and fast. Made me wanna stay hurt so I could get this treatment all the time.

"You know I love you right?" Tre asked while massaging my feet.

"Yeah, boy."

I felt butterflies. I hadn't felt that in so long, it scared me. I didn't want to, but I fell deeper for him in that moment. Even after all the shit we had been through, I couldn't help myself.

12

THIS MEANS WAR

KIA

Fear washed over me as I was snatched up as soon as I walked into my house. Out of all the days when Rico chose not be home, it had to be this one. I had just returned from my Cuba trip with the girls only to come home to three masked men in the house I shared with one of the 'most feared' men in the game. Pssh! Obviously, somebody wasn't scared because here I was, being abducted and carted off to some place I had never seen before. I screamed as loud as I could, but nobody heard me. I looked out of the window in terror as Jas pulled off. I was doomed.

I had been crying so hard, my head hurt. My nose was clogged but running at the same time. My throat hurt so bad. Whoever had me had enough decency to at least wipe my eyes and nose. The blindfold had finally been removed and I was in a huge room surrounded by paintings and other works of art. It was beautiful and all, but what the fuck was I doing here? I hadn't been able to think clearly but as soon as I had a moment, the conclusion became clear as day. I was about to die.

Somehow, this was the consequence of Dro's death. I was certain they were trying to get back at Rico and I was fuckin' collateral. It was no doubt in my mind now that I knew Rico had in fact killed Dro.

This would be too much of a coincidence for me to get kidnapped out of the blue. I didn't have any beef in the streets, especially not with people who were capable of this sort of thing. Rico was the only one.

I silently cursed him as I scanned the room for a way out or a damn clue as to who exactly had me here. I was assed out. I was tied to the chair, couldn't move, and I was slowly coming to grips with the fact that it was over for me. The good thing was, I would be reunited with Dro sooner than I thought. I knew my baby was in heaven waiting for me. I had been so depressed since learning he was dead, that I didn't really care what happened at this point. If I lived, I would forever be left with the heartache. Death would be better than staring the person who killed my soulmate in the eyes every day. I was ready.

After a while, I heard someone enter the room. Their footsteps grew closer and closer. I knew the time was coming, so I bowed my head and prayed my final prayer. "God please forgive me for my sins," I mouthed before I felt the killer behind me.

TRE

Life had gone back to normal for the time being, but I was about to seriously fuck some shit up again. I had been watching my brother like a hawk. Him and that freak-bitch Tiffany had been real cozy. From my point of view, it looked like love. Every time I saw her nasty ass I would start singing the lyrics to Playboi Carti, *wokeuplikethis* "Dat bitch dat you wifin', she so triflin'" and laugh to myself. That disrespectful-ass bird had the nerve to be actin' like she was just so innocent around my brother. Her dirty little secret was about to be revealed.

I had been waiting in the cut for the perfect moment to do the unthinkable. It was almost that time. That nigga had actually been ring shopping. He was really about to pop the question to this smut. Part of me knew this was revenge, but the other part felt like I was saving him. This bitch ain't deserve no ring. I mean maybe from another nigga but not from my brother.

Part of me wanted to let him wife the hoe. Shit, we done all fell for one, or five. It wouldn't be his first time though. I just knew he was gonna kill that girl after this and that was the only thing that was making me hesitant. I mean, Ava was still alive after he found out about us, but she did have his two children. I didn't want to be responsible for the death of any woman, in any way. That wasn't my MO, but I just had to show this nigga that he couldn't touch me, and that I could still touch him.

He thought he was invincible because of his line of work. Sure, the nigga was feared, but not by me. I knew one man that *he* feared, and that was my dad.

"Aye, Pop, you know yo' son about to get engaged right?"

"Look here, leave that boy alone before he snaps for real. He already crazy as shit," my pops said.

He knew me so well.

"I am gonna leave him alone. Right after this last thing."

"I'll tell you like I told him, anything happens to either one of you, you gonna regret the day you were born."

"A'ight, man, I'm gone. I got shit to do." I hurriedly left his house after a short visit turned into an hour and a threat on my life.

I still had my plan and my father wasn't gonna stop this. I didn't know what was gonna happen afterward, but at this point, I gave no fucks. I was on a path of destruction and nobody could stop me. Just as I was about to pull up to Marcus' house and destroy his soul, my phone rang, and the call knocked the wind outta me.

CHASE

"Wait, what? Isabella calm down and explain this shit to me!"

"Bitch, you heard me! Your fuckin' girlfriend called me and told me she was pregnant by you. Now you know we over, right?" She smiled wickedly.

"Doggg, what the fuck are you talkin' about? I ain't got no bitch pregnant."

"Really, does this number look familiar? You know who the fuck Kalani is, right? The girl you been fuckin' since before we even got together," she screamed while smashing her phone into my face.

"Mannn, ain't no way she pregnant by me, g."

"Why the fuck not? You know you been fuckin' her. And I dare you lie in my face bitch," she threatened.

"She on birth control," I mumbled.

"Well clearly she lied cuz the hoe pregnant. Good luck with that," she said patting my shoulder and walking out.

This was her house, but she was leaving. I was halfway scared to death cuz Isabella usually wanted to fight. She was too calm this time, which meant she was prolly done wit' my ass for good. Once again, my dick had gotten me into trouble. I quickly hopped in my car and sped home. Kalani had been staying with me since she had been in Detroit.

"So, you pregnant," I asked as soon as I saw her sitting there.

"Yeah."

"So, instead of telling me, you go and tell my baby mama?"

"Yeah," she smiled.

What the fuck was this? Why were all these bitches smiling like some shit was amusing about this situation.

"What the fuck so funny?"

"Nothin'," she shrugged.

I wasn't happy with all these one-word answers.

"How the hell you get pregnant on birth control?"

"I must have lied," she told me, standing.

She didn't give a fuck either.

"So, basically you trapped me?"

"Basically." She nodded her head.

"Bitch, get the fuck out!" I finally snapped but instead of putting my hands on her, I stepped to the side and let her walk out.

"Where am I supposed to go?"

"The fuck away from me. Here's some money for a hotel." I handed her a wad of cash and she reluctantly left.

The next couple weeks were pure hell. Both of my bitches were gone. I ain't have no hoes and I was horny as fuck. That shit was wild how my life could go from sugar to shit in a matter of one bad decision. I mean, I knew I shouldn't have fucked with Kalani, but I did. I didn't expect her to do no shit like this. This wasn't even in her character. I guess I pushed her too far.

My doorbell ringing snapped me from my thoughts. It was Ronnie. I figured he was here about some work, so I went to let him in. When I opened the door, I realized it wasn't just Ronnie. It was him and his boys. They were all scowling which meant they came here to do some damage. Before I could say anything, they rushed me.

"Aye, you got my li'l sister pregnant and put her out? And you thought I wasn't gon' find out?" Ronnie yelled as he punched and kicked me.

She must have called them immediately. I could take a beating though. As long as these niggas didn't kill me, I would be okay. I hoped he knew that his connect I supplied him with was gone now because of this. I mean, I knew I was wrong, but she was just as wrong as I was. Nobody told her ass to lie.

As they were kicking and punching, I was easing back further toward my coffee table with the gun underneath. They were so busy beatin' my ass that they didn't notice I was reaching for it until I was too late. Before I could get to my gun, I heard shots ringing all around me. I just knew I was dead now.

ISABELLA

I was hurt as hell and crying profusely as I sat a few houses from Chase. I had come here to fuck his ass up one last time before I disappeared. I sat there and thought long and hard about my next move. I felt all types of stupid for being in this situation, for caring and for feeling like I pushed him to fuck with that girl. I knew something had to be wrong for me to be even considering blaming myself for a man's actions and in that instance, I knew I needed to pull the fuck off.

The only problem was I couldn't even drive I was so paralyzed with rage and anger. I didn't know what to do. I wanted to kill him to be honest, but I couldn't. I at least could beat his ass for the one time. I finally worked up the strength to call Jas.

"Bitch, please come here now. I'm about to kill this nigga," I sobbed into the phone.

"What? Where?"

"I'm sending you the location now."

She got here so fast and threw me a pair of Timbs. I guess this was customary for her because it certainly wasn't her first time. I laughed as I laced them up and we prepared to run up in his crib. What I saw next, stopped us dead in our tracks. Three men had entered his house and there was a heap of commotion.

I heard somebody yell, "You got my lil' sister pregnant and put her out!" Then I heard more loud bangs and shit falling over. Now, we were no dummies, we weren't about to just run up in there like we were gangsta. Both Jas and I popped our trunks and grabbed a weapon. Fuckin' with these types of men, you always had to be strapped.

We crept up to the house slowly and noticed that Chase was getting the shit beat out of him. I wanted to laugh because he honestly deserved it, but when I saw one of them pulling a gun, it was over. We both let off shots clearing that shit before they took my baby daddy out the game for real. I don't care how much I hated him, nobody was gonna kill him but me.

Jas called Tre and told him to get here. We couldn't call an ambulance because we'd all be going to prison. I tried to nurse Chase as much as I could. His bloody mouth caused him not to be able to talk as easily, but I did hear him say, "Call Ficks." That was the doctor that he had back in Cali when I got shot. How the fuck was he gonna get here fast enough?

I called anyway, and he put me in contact with a 'specialist' in the area and I quickly made the call. The same time Tre arrived, so did the van that came the last time there was a scene this gruesome. I never thought in a million years that I'd be exposed to some shit like this, but here I was, used to the shit. I knew the procedure and protocol too.

"The fuck happened?" Tre asked us as he sat down and sparked a blunt amidst the chaos.

There was spraying, bleaching, carpet and body removal going on around us and he was so cool about it. I guess when you lived that life, you become immune to it.

"Well, he got some girl pregnant, put her out, and then her brother and his weak-ass goons came." I shrugged.

"Damn, he out here like that?" He took a few pulls then passed it to Jas.

"I guess so. He did say she lied and said she was on birth control, which the bitch confirmed when she called again. I don't know why bitches do this type of shit."

"That's crazy. And I guess y'all two the pink and yellow power rangers huh." He chuckled like we ain't just save his punk-ass brother's life.

"Thelma and Louise," I laughed.

Jas was quiet as fuck smoking all the blunt and not even passin' it.

"Baby, can somebody else hit it?" Tre tapped her, and she jumped.

"You okay," I asked, thinkin' she was mad at Tre.

"Bitch, no, the police outside."

13

THE TRUTH SHALL SET YOU FREE

SIMONE

Planning my wedding was so beautiful. I don't see how women turn into bridezillas and started yelling and screaming at everyone. My shit was smooth as hell. I had found the venue. Well, my wedding planner did. I had found the perfect dress. My bridesmaids had been notified and all except Kia had responded and had gone to get fitted for their dresses. The cake was being designed by this amazing cake lady I found on Instagram.

All of my pre-wedding events were planned, and invites had been sent. This shit was seamless. I had even met up with Jas to get her opinion on some things. We had ended up talking about Kia in the process.

"So, do you think she'll be able to make it to the wedding, even if she isn't a bridesmaid?"

"Girl, if she came to your baby shower, of course she's gonna come to the wedding," she chuckled. "She's just going through some shit right now, you know? I'm tryna give her some space but it's been days since I spoke to her. I'm gonna go by there tomorrow and make sure she's okay. You should come with."

"I will. I need to talk to my girl. I know how bad I took it when

Kalief got shot. She gotta be hurt as hell with the situation she was in."

"I couldn't imagine, sis. So, how's the wedding planning?"

"Easier than I thought. I don't know, maybe it's because of the event planner or that I'm not doing anything extravagant."

"I can't believe that," Jas laughed.

"Well believe it. I'm doin' it a little small. I just want it to be safe cuz my baby boy will be there, and you remember what happened last time."

"I'll never forget."

"Girl, no matter how hard I try, I can't get that image out of my mind. This dark figure just standing there, waiting to strike as soon as the doors open. Like, who the hell was that and what was their issue with *me*? I've never done anything to anyone. At least not enough for them to exact that type of revenge."

"I know. Is anyone looking into that? Did they check with security? Camera footage?"

"Yep, they have the person on camera, but nobody knows anything in particular and all of the searches keep coming up with nothing. Whoever it was, they were small, so it's hard to come to a conclusion on who it could be. Any nigga that they possibly have beef with is at least twice that person's size."

"That's wild. I'm just glad you're okay. You've been through a helluva lot." Jas hugged me tight as we prepared to say our goodbyes.

I was so glad she came to hang out with me. I had been missing her company. Now only if I could get Kia to text back or something, all would be right in the holy trinity that was our friendship. The wedding was in a few weeks and I needed her to be fitted for her gown and participate in the festivities. If she wasn't there, I wasn't gonna feel right. She was always there no matter what.

THE NEXT MORNING, Jas was at my house bright and early so we could go check on Kia. I left KJ with his father and joined her in the car. We headed to her old house first, and of course she wasn't there. We just wanted to check in case she went there to clear her head of ratchet Rico. Next, we travelled to the home they shared together.

We happened to see Rico outside. Perfect timing.

"Where's Kia?" we asked in unison.

He had this weird look on his face that showed us that he didn't know, but it wasn't good.

"Is she okay? Is she missing," I asked in a panicky tone.

I was getting worried as fuck because that expression he wore meant he was hiding something.

"Y'all might wanna come in and sit down," he told us, ushering us inside his house.

I was already on the verge of tears.

"Get to it," Jas demanded.

"A'ight, so I guess after y'all man-hatin' trip y'all take every five minutes, somebody must have got her. I mean obviously she came back with y'all. I was gone but when I got here, there was this note and Kia wasn't here." He handed us a note that said, "She's not coming home."

My heart skipped a beat. Jas' leg was shaking profusely as she tried to hold back tears.

"Rico what the fuck did you do!?" She got up, screaming and yelling in his face about Dro and all this other shit that was foreign to me.

I mean, I knew Kia and Dro had a relationship, but she had asked him if he killed Dro and that was something I hadn't heard yet. This shit was unfolding right in front of me and I was quickly piecing together the puzzle.

"You killed him now they got my best friend! If anything happens to her, I swear to *God!*" Through gritted teeth she kept cursing and threatening his life.

I was scared for him because I knew Jas didn't play about Kia. She would fuck anybody up over her best friend, hell, we all would.

"Listen, I fucked up," Rico admitted as he broke down in tears right along with Jas.

He knew what that note meant and it was all bad for Kia. I started to imagine life without her. All the years we had shared, the heartache and heartbreak we had talked each other through and I almost had a nervous breakdown. All three of us were crying our eyes out. Rico was on his knees hugging Jas around the waist, apologizing for all the fucked-up shit he did. It was all bad for all of us.

JASMINE

After what seemed like hours of crying, I finally peeled myself off the floor and went home. Simone came with me because neither of us were in the position mentally to be alone. We prayed all the way there and all throughout the night that Kia was safe no matter how bad it looked.

Against my will, I answered the phone when Tre called me at about one-thirty in the morning. I was groggy and tired as hell from crying.

"Baby, I'm outside, open the door," he said and hung up.

I could barely get myself out of bed. Once I made it to the door, to my surprise both Tre and Kalief were on the other side.

"Come in y'all."

Simone had stirred from her sleep when she heard her man at the door. I thought their relationship was so adorable. I had never seen them argue and it was always a good vibe. They realized they had each been through too much to be hating each other. That's something Tre needed to learn if we were ever gonna be together. Yeah, I said it.

He followed me to my room and I plopped down on the bed,

ready to cuddle and probably cry some more. He scooted behind me and held me tightly, kissing my cheeks and neck.

"Tre," I called, trying to stop him from turning this sexual.

"I know already, we on it. You don't need to talk about it no more tonight. We got people lookin' for her. She's gonna be fine," he reassured me.

"But what if—," he cut me off again.

"Trust me baby, she's gonna be fine.

"How the fuck do *you* know? Huh? She could be somewhere dead as we speak and it's all because of your bitch-ass homeboy!" I had started the waterworks again.

I cried 'til I was hoarse. He did everything he could to comfort me, but nothing worked.

"Jasmine, listen, I know how it looks. I know how fucked-up it is and how it was Rico's fault. But what can you do right now? We have no idea where she is or who took her, but we got somebody making sense of this shit as we speak. Can we please revisit this in the morning?"

"Fuck you, bitch."

"Take yo' pills and relax."

That was insensitive as fuck, but I surely did take my pill. I needed it to relax and make me sleep. It was sad that at times I was dependent on drugs to make me sleep. After I swallowed the pills with some water, Tre was there rubbing my back with chamomile oil, just how I liked it. After that shit kicked in, he knew exactly what to do. He kept rubbing and palming this ass 'til he heard me moaning softly beneath him.

He lifted my t-shirt, exposing my nakedness and started to suck my right nipple while gently playing with the left. He knew that shit drove me crazy, which is why that was always his go-to to get my defenses down. Nipple stimulation orgasms were a thing and he made sure I got mine. I lost all my inhibitions and for once that day, I wasn't worried about anything. I didn't have a care in the world.

However, the following day, anxiety set in as soon as I woke up and heard Tre's phone call. There was no word on where Kia was, who she was with or if she was coming back. My mind raced a mile a minute as I grabbed my phone and started to blow hers up. After getting no answer, I shot her a text.

Please Ki, if you all right, text me back.

MARCUS

Shit was crazy. I knew I was movin' fast, but love like this didn't come around often. It was a point in time when I thought I'd never love again. Every woman I encountered was just bad for me. No matter how much I had given them, I just couldn't get anything in return. I had been through that scenario with three different women.

I wasn't perfect at all. I mean, I killed people for a living, I sold drugs and even did drugs for a minute, but when I loved, I loved for real. I would've done anything for Ava. Even though there was a time I fell severely off my game with her, I bounced back. And what did she do? Go and fuck my brother. Same with Isabella. I treated her with nothing but respect, she just couldn't stop being a hoe to save her life. Then Nakita. I really thought that bitch loved me. After all, I had rescued her from her husband who was cheating on her and look what she did? Ran right back to the nigga.

That's why I killed people. Because they deserve it. You go around hurting people because of your own selfish needs and next thing you know, your body being cleaned up out of a warehouse by some niggas I hired. One day muhfuckas might learn their lesson, maybe not, but you were gonna suffer your karma. One way or another, you would reap what you sowed.

I snapped myself from my angry thoughts and tried to focus on the plans I had for tonight. I was inviting Tiffany over for a special dinner. I had it catered because a nigga ain't wanna fuck up the moment with some burnt-ass food. With the way my mind was racing, I woulda burned the whole house down if I tried to cook.

I had every hood nigga favorite meal: lamb chops, lobster tails, shrimp, mac and cheese, asparagus and biscuits. That shit was smellin' so good I almost couldn't wait for her to get here. I had about fifteen minutes before she was to arrive, so I rehearsed what I was gonna say to her a few more times before my phone vibrated. It was an attachment from an unknown number.

What I saw when I opened it made me wanna vomit. I threw the phone and it shattered into a million pieces. I tried and tried to maintain my cool, but it was in vain. I threw everything in my path, ruining my whole kitchen and living room in a matter of minutes. The damage I had caused would take actual repairmen to fix.

Seconds later, I heard Tiffany using her key to open the front door. She walked in, calling my name in a panic. I guess she had surveyed the mess. When she found me, she immediately started asking me what was wrong, as if she didn't know. Since she wanted to play with me, I grabbed her around her neck and choked her lifeless. I left her body right there on the floor and went to take a shower. It was over for my brother.

SIMONE

Despite everything that had taken place, my wedding was still happening. I had talked to Jas and she urged me to keep my date and time and that everything would be okay. I took her word and continued with my planning. Everything was perfect on my big day. This was the day that I would finally get to marry the man I had been in love with for so long.

I felt bad that Kia wasn't here to share this day. Wherever she was, I kept praying that she was safe and sound and out of harm's way. Maybe she staged that shit and ran off somewhere. That was the latest scenario I used to cope with her disappearance. She was somewhere on an island clearing her head of all the drama back home.

I said my final prayer over her and continued to be pampered. It seemed like I'd just been living the life. I had a beautiful baby boy, I had a blessed birthday and got proposed to, now I'm at my wedding about to marry this amazing man that cares more about me than I do for myself. With all the pain I'd suffered, he'd been there to make it bearable. Without him, I don't know where I would be. Probably dead since he's the one that saved me from jumping off the ledge that day.

Damn, we had been through it all. Not to mention all the crazy shit we had experienced as friends. I was there when they first got in the drug game. From shootouts, to stick-ups to beating cases and all. We had a crazy history, but our future was gonna be lit as fuck.

After preparing myself for hours, I was finally ready. My gown which featured a five-foot train, swept the floor. It was sheer and encrusted with Swarovski crystals. Some people said they were shocked I was wearing a white dress when my favorite color was black. I decided to go the traditional route, but at least my décor was black.

It was finally time for me to be reunited with my love after not seeing him for a few days. We followed *all* the wedding traditions and superstitions. The music cued, I gave myself the once over in the hallway before entering and I almost cried at how beautiful I was. My makeup was so flawless, I looked natural. My veil couldn't even cover how gorgeous I looked underneath.

It was time for me to walk and I sauntered effortlessly to the music. Kalief's dad was giving me away seeing as I had killed mine and he would be no good alive anyway. My mom was there though, sitting close to the front, crying her eyes out. Then my eyes spotted someone familiar and I swear I almost fuckin' fainted.

KIA

"God please forgive me for my sins," I mouthed before I felt the killer behind me.

They walked around to the side of me, cut the ropes that bound my hands and feet then stepped to the front. I was too afraid to even look up. Then I felt a hand on my chin, urging me to open my eyes and come face-to-face with the person that was about to end my life.

"Damien," I cried as I finally laid eyes on him.

I jumped into his arms, weeping and sobbing like a mad woman.

"I thought you were dead! Why the fuck didn't you answer the phone?"

"Calm down. I fuckin' missed you dog," he exclaimed wasting no time shoving his tongue down my throat.

We made love so terribly, I knew I would be sore the next day, but I didn't give a fuck. I needed him so bad that it hurt my heart more.

I was relieved to know I wasn't dying. But the feeling that came over me knowing that my man was alive and well caused me to cry every minute. I kept repeating myself over and over, until he finally shushed me and told me not to say that I thought he was dead again. I knew I had said the shit like fifty times, but nigga, I really truly believed in my heart that he was gone.

I was so lost in Dro for the past few weeks that I hadn't even considered that my friends and family may have been worried about me. I had finally turned my phone back on and had hundreds of missed calls and texts. When I found Jas' I immediately text her that I was okay. We talked for a while and I filled her in on what happened and begged her not to tell anybody.

In the midst of our conversation, she mentioned Simone's wedding and I knew I had to show my face again for that. I figured Rico wouldn't show up because he was probably too busy looking for me to be out celebrating anything.

I got the shock of my life when we locked eyes just as Simone entered the room. Then the second look which was the 'I saw a ghost' face when he saw me sitting next to Dro. He couldn't do shit, but be seated because I knew he wasn't about to ruin Simone's wedding, especially with what went on at the shower. He couldn't keep still though, and I was laughing inside knowing that his shitty plan had backfired, and he was forced to sit there while his love was still with the man he tried to kill.

Aside from that, the ceremony had us all in tears. I kept having to strain my neck because some bitch decided to wear a big-ass church hat. I mean, you couldn't even see this bitch's face that hat was so big. Unbeknownst to us all, when the minister asked if anyone objected to their union, her ass stood right up, and she had a gun pointed straight at Simone.

KALIEF

I had waited for this day for so long. I knew since the day I met Simone, that she was gonna be mine. Life got in the way for a long time, but today was the day that it was finally happening. All of the events that occurred up until this time, whether good or bad, had helped us get to this point. It made us strong and it made our bond stronger. Marrying Simone was the best idea I had ever come up with.

Most of all, our family was perfect. Although I had a child from a previous relationship, my daughter Jayla loved Simone and Simone loved Jayla just as much, you would've thought Simone was Jayla's birth mom judging by how close their relationship was. Now, of course this didn't sit too well with her mother, Kema, but she should've been happy that I found someone that loved our daughter just as much as we did.

I had custody of Jayla though, so it didn't matter what anyone thought. We were a family now, and nobody could stop that. That was until the minister asked if anyone objected. I expected crickets, so I didn't even notice the woman in the big church hat that rose to her feet holding a gun. She pointed it straight at Simone with the same posture and trembling hand as the person who slashed her face that day at the baby shower.

I will never forget that as long as I live. That's why I immediately sprang into action. This bitch wasn't gonna get away with hurting her again. I heard the gunshots let off while I was hopping over people and the pews to tackle this crazed woman in the crowd. I had successfully taken her down and wrestled the gun from her. I snatched off that big-ass church hat and saw none other than my baby mama. I screamed for someone to call an ambulance.

"Kema?"

I didn't know what to do at this point. This was the mother of my child. She had clearly lost her mind in a jealous rage. I had no idea why I didn't think it was her from the beginning. She could've easily gotten the information out of Jayla about the baby shower and the wedding. Now it was too late, and my baby was shot, laying in a pool of blood while I fought with my psycho baby mama for the gun she kept trying to get.

She had it in her hand while I struggled to get it from her. You know they say crazy people have superhuman strength. It was true because the next thing I knew; this bitch had blown her own brains out.

My mouth hung open as I let her lifeless body fall to the floor and blood started to pour from her head, mouth and nose. This wasn't happening. My child's mother had just killed herself and possibly my wife at our wedding. I couldn't even process it. Everything from that point on was a blur. I couldn't even tell you what happened after that point. All I kept seeing was a continuous loop of Kema standing up with the gun, shooting Simone and then shooting herself.

14

SILENCE IS GOLDEN

TRE

F UCK! I yelled internally as I kept getting Jas' voicemail. She had promised me that she wasn't gon' disappear on me again, and here she was, gone with no word. After what had happened to her best friend Simone, I found it odd that she would just go missing like that when her friend was in the hospital fighting for her life. Something was up but I thought that maybe she just couldn't handle it and her, Kia and Isabella had run off somewhere. It was pretty heartless, but that's exactly what those bitches were, pretty and heartless. Speaking of Kia, while we were all happy she was alive, nobody but those three thought her littler stunt was cute. I don't know who was more pissed between Rico, Chase and me.

Speak of the devil, as soon as I think of them three bitches, I get a call from none other than the devil herself, Isabella.

"Tre, please don't hang up," she said, sounding like she was crying.

"What's wrong, what happened?"

"I can't get in touch with Chase and it's an emergency."

"Aye, you with Jas?"

"No, that's another thing. Me or Kia hasn't heard from her and she's not at home. Tre, please tell Chase to get here, now!"

"A'ight I got you."

I hung up and called my brother.

"Aye bro, you gotta get to yo' baby mama. She scared and cryin' and told me it's an emergency."

"A'ight, I'm on my way. Good lookin.'"

Some shit was definitely up. Whenever she dipped, she always had Isabella with her, now all of a sudden, she's gone with no word and no partner in crime. Now that I thought about it, I had fucked-up and left the door wide open for Jas to be in grave danger. If I didn't get to her in time, it wouldn't be her fighting for her life, she wouldn't have one to fight for.

CHASE

I hopped in my car and sped all the way to Isabella's. I remembered I had blocked her and that's why she couldn't get in contact with me. I quickly dialed her number on the way there to try and prepare myself for what could have possibly happened. She answered on the first ring like she was expecting my call.

"Baby, is everything okay?"

"No, Chase," she sobbed into the phone.

"What's wrong? Tell me what happened."

"Just get here please. I don't know what to do with this bitch."

I knew the worst had happened and my fears were confirmed when I got to Isabella's house and found Kalani bleeding out with her eyes wide open.

"What the fuck happened?" I asked her as I surveyed the gruesome scene.

"I don't know how this bitch found out where I lived, but she came to my house. I don't know why she wanted to talk to me about you. I told her I didn't care but she was determined to make me give a fuck."

"That's not telling me what happened," I pressured. I wanted to know why she was lying there lifeless and staring at the ceiling.

"She threatened to go to the police about her brother, so I made all of our lives easier. I just sent her straight to her brother," she shrugged, staring into space.

I had never heard some gangsta shit spoken so eloquently. I knew in that instant that Isabella and I were meant for each other and we were gonna be together for a long-ass time, if not forever. She was my soulmate, my evil twin. She still had my back regardless of what we went through, and I was grateful for that.

"I love you, Isabella DeMichael," I randomly blurted out.

"I love you too, Chase," she admitted with a sigh.

"You know no matter what, you can call me and I'm glad you did."

"I know."

Even though I knew repairing what I had broken wasn't gonna be easy, at least there was hope. I knew she still loved me and that was a start. It was crazy that we were bonding over a dead body, but I wouldn't trade this moment for the world. Knowing my girl still had my back meant everything to me. Knowing she would catch a body for ya boy meant that she still cared even though I couldn't always tell.

After cleaning up the scene, I took her home with me. Her, the baby, and her mom. I didn't want them in that house after what happened. It felt so good to have my family under one roof again. I would do anything to keep things exactly as they were, but more trouble soon followed.

ISABELLA

"So, nobody has heard from Jas?" I asked as the whole crew huddled together in Tre's living room.

"Nope," they all replied in unison.

This wasn't good. Jas never disappeared like this without me. By the look on Tre's face, he knew something that the rest of us didn't. I couldn't help but to notice how uneasy and afraid he looked the whole time. I mean, I knew that was his girl and all, but he had an immense amount of worry that was radiating from him. He knew she was in some sort of trouble.

"Tre, speak up," I finally said after I had enough of him fidgeting.

"I know exactly where she is. I mean, not where, but *who* has her."

"Who? Why haven't you told anybody?"

"Because, I have to handle this. If anything happens to Jas, I don't know what I'm gonna do." I knew he was serious and whatever situation she was in was dangerous.

"Who has her, Tre?" I asked again, since he conveniently skipped that part.

"Marcus." When he uttered that name, I wanted to die.

I had barely escaped from him in the past and I knew all that he was capable of. He was a menace and with all that had gone on between Tre and Marcus, I knew he was out for blood. I immediately started thinking the worst. With *that* nigga, Jas could already be dead. He had no remorse for anyone or anything that he did. He was a cold-blooded killing machine with no conscience.

Tears started to form in my eyes and everyone noticed. Only a few people knew what I had suffered dealing with Marcus, but everyone knew who he was and what he was about. My heart was thumping out of my chest as I stood there trying to regulate my breathing. I felt the air being sucked right out of my lungs as that revelation caused me to relive one of the scariest moments of my life. That coupled with what I had recently gone through with having to shoot that damn girl and my head was spinning.

Everything became cloudy and my chest started to tighten up. I was having a panic attack right there in front of everybody. All I remember is Chase catching me before I fell and then I woke up in a hospital room.

"Thank God," Chase sighed when my eyes fluttered open.

Once again, he was there for me.

"What happened, baby?" I asked. I was confused when I realized where I was.

"Man, you had some type of anxiety attack. How do you feel?"

"Like I need to get out of here," I said, suddenly remembering why I was here in the first place. "Is anyone checking on Jasmine? Has anyone heard from her?"

"Calm down. Tre is on it as we speak," he reassured me.

JASMINE

For the last two days I had been sitting in this musty-ass room with dim lights and the smell of death surrounding me. The dripping from the pipes in the molded ceiling was driving me crazy but I hadn't lost it just yet. I was quietly plotting my escape the whole time while he thought I was going along with his sick-ass plan.

I don't give a fuck how down and out I seem, I'm always plotting and the weak bitch he paired up with was about to see exactly who the fuck she was playin' with. Every time me and this bitch, Tiffany, were alone, she would brag about how she fucked my man and all this worthless bullshit. But little did she know, I had a plan for her ass too.

"If you had him so open, why aren't you with him now?" I asked during my supervised shower.

Isabella told me about her experience being kidnapped before and it was scary just to hear. Never would I ever think that I would be in the same fuckin' predicament. I'm glad I listened because I was able to have some type of idea of what was to come. It aided me in figuring out my escape. I knew exactly what I needed to do to get out of there. I just hoped everything work out like I had planned.

"Bitch, mind yours," she spat.

"So, you chose to be with a fuckin' maniac who beats the shit out of you and makes you babysit other women who he plans to kill? You signed up to be an accessory to murder? You're a nurse for God sakes." I laid it on thick, hoping to strike a nerve so I could quickly make my next move.

See, Marcus made a big mistake by giving this bitch a phone. Yeah, her mindless ass wasn't gonna call the police, but that didn't have shit to do with me. If I could just get to the phone while holding her back, I would be good as rescued.

"That's your last fuckin' strike! Hurry up so I can take you to Marcus."

"You're so pathetic. This man doesn't even want you and you're doing all his dirty work. Incriminating yourself just to be down. Bitches like you end up in one of two places, dead or in jail," I said, laughing at her stupidity.

I was surprised she didn't even attack me as I started putting on my clothes. I was pissed because I needed her to come at me first for my plan to work. Seeing that she wouldn't budge, while she kept that prissy-ass smirk on her face, made my blood boil. When she walked in front of me to unlock the bathroom door, I snapped. I grabbed that bitch by her ponytail and slammed her head into the porcelain sink. I rammed and rammed her shit until I saw blood leaking.

That shit still didn't knock her out. She still had some fight left in her. Some way, she knocked me onto the floor and was now on top of me. That's what snortin' them lines did to you, gave you superpowers, cuz it was no way this bitch should've still been conscious. She was throwing blows and missing most of them while I struggled with her heavy-ass body on top of me.

"Bitch," she screamed as she clawed at my face.

We were truly fighting to the death and she was unfortunately winning at the moment. I was tasting blood as she continued her assault on my face. She had started to choke me, and I tussled to escape her grip. The bitch was strong! I eased my leg up and used my knee to knock her in her chin so hard her head hit the sink, temporarily allowing me the upper-hand. It was no more games after that. I swiftly rose to my feet, dizzy and bleeding, took my shirt off and wrapped it around her neck.

I squeezed so tight I could see her eyes bulging from the top of her head. After a few minutes, I let her lifeless body drop to the floor. I quickly found the phone and it was on three percent. I was now faced with the hardest decision of my life. Call the police or call Tre.

MARCUS

"You a tough cookie," I chuckled as Tre's little girlfriend sat there stone-faced during her mild torture. "You must really love that nigga."

"Fuck him and you," she spat.

"Now, that's not nice." I smiled before I reared my hand back and slapped her across her face.

She was all bruised and bloody but that's what happened when you had a smart-ass mouth. She was lucky I hadn't killed her yet. Honestly, I didn't know if I wanted to kill her or recruit her ass after witnessing what she did to Tiffany in that bathroom. A bitch that lethal needed to be on the team, but I didn't think she would want to be down with her loyalty to my brother and all.

What I *was* gonna do was get me a taste of that pussy though. Just for a little payback. Since my brother was always stickin' his dick in one of my bitches, I thought it was time I returned the favor. I didn't wanna fuck the bitch all bloody and shit, so I helped her get cleaned up. I stood behind her while she washed the dried blood and mucus from her nose.

"You still beautiful even wit' yo face like that," I told her.

I meant it too. Jas was a gorgeous girl and her strength made her even more attractive. Look at me, catchin' feelings. I had to laugh internally.

"Fuck you," she spat, elbowing me lightly in the stomach. "Back up off me. I'm not Tiffany."

"I know you ain't. You ain't no weak-ass bitch. You hold yo' own and I gotta respect that. I will warn you, though. I'm also not Tiffany," I reminded her.

"What the fuck do you want with me?"

"You my brother's girl and I gotta teach him a lesson sweetheart. Hate it had to be you. You got so much potential."

"So, what are you gonna do? Keep me here forever? He's not even here for you to teach a lesson to," she scoffed.

"That should show you that he doesn't give a fuck about you then, right?"

"No, it shows me you ain't got the balls to call him here cuz you know what would happen."

"That's cute. I swear, I like you. You the type of bitch I need in my life. You vicious."

"You have no idea."

"I do. My bro told me a little bit about you. I know this ain't yo first body."

"And it won't be my last either."

"You makin' my dick hard," I told her as I sat down and prepared to treat my nose.

"Have some," I offered, and she refused, but I wasn't taking no for an answer.

I pulled my gun out and cocked it. After a short stand-off, she finally did what I asked and snorted the lines I sat out for her. After a little bit, she was relaxed and out of it, allowing me to have my way. I picked her up and placed her on the table we had just got high on and started to kiss on her. I wanted to make sure she was all the way there. By her response, she was.

I dropped my gun on the floor to the side of me and pulled her closer to me. I lifted her top, exposing her perfect set of titties and started to suck one at a time. Hearing her moans excited me and made my dick even harder than it was. Just as I was about to penetrate, I got the shock of my life.

TRE

"Dog, what the fuck," I barked as I approached my brother.

He had my girl ass-naked with her legs wide open. I was fiery mad. I knew she was under pressure, but I never thought she would allow this shit to happen. Then I saw it. I saw the coke residue and the gun that lay next to his feet and realized he must have forced her to get high. I was about to kill this nigga in cold blood. I cocked my gun and held it toward his head.

"Don't do this," my dad said, placing his hand over the gun and lowering it.

I had brought him along because he seemed to be the only one who could reason with Marcus. If it was just us, one of us would be dead and it wouldn't be me.

Marcus quickly pulled himself together and tried to go for his gun, but I stopped that shit. I kicked it away before he would get to it.

"Get the fuck back, nigga." I shoved him away from Jas and helped to put her clothes back on while Marcus sheepishly looked away from my dad.

He had the nerve to be embarrassed and hang his head in shame. He knew this was not what my father wanted for him when he bestowed the hitman job title upon him.

"Marky, what the fuck are you doin'?" my dad bellowed, causing Marcus to jump.

"Don't call me no fuckin' Marky!"

"You better answer me, boy." He gritted his teeth as he spoke.

"Getting revenge."

"And this is what you call revenge? Kidnapping some girl and raping her?"

"This ain't his first time," I added.

My dad looked so disappointed in him and Marcus looked equally ashamed.

I had removed Jas off the table and just hugged her while she could barely stand up or stay still. I still had my gun pointed at Marcus. I knew better because that nigga was quick and always had a trick up his sleeve.

"Yeah, hug that bitch cuz I already fucked her," he laughed maniacally.

That was it. I kindly let go of Jas and came at this nigga full force. He had that coke high, so he was stronger than usual. My father yelled for us to stop from the sidelines, but I couldn't. He had crossed the line. I was about to put a bullet in this niggas mouth for old time's sake.

We continued to struggle, knocking down everything in our path. Marcus had a strong grip on the gun and was slowly turning it away from his mouth, where I had aimed it.

"That's enough," I heard my dad yell from right over us.

He was trying to pull me off him but to no avail. Jas couldn't help because she was so out of it. She just sat there on the dirty ground, rocking back and forth, enjoying her high. I don't know what she could've done to stop him anyway, but I silently prayed that this nigga lost his grip, or my dad pushed him off. I knew he didn't want either of us hurt. He really didn't know what to do in this situation.

Then I saw Jas moving toward Marcus' gun. Everything flashed before my eyes. I didn't want her to kill him. If anyone was gonna kill him, it was me. I started to panic. Marcus kept twisting the gun further and further toward me and I tried my best to counteract it, but my strength paled in comparison to his cocaine-induced superpowers. *Pop!* The gun went off and I felt blood splatter all over me. Did this nigga really just shoot me?

EPILOGUE

Huddled over the tombstone, I watched Tre cry his eyes out. I had never witnessed him this broken and vulnerable before. I tried my best to comfort him, but he was taking this loss to the heart and no amount of consoling would help. After that day, that fateful day that ended his father's life, Tre had been a different person.

He and Marcus couldn't bury the hatchet, so instead, they buried their father. Tre Sr. was the man responsible for creating the monster that was his son. He ultimately was the reason Marcus turned out to be the savage that he was. And for that, he paid. He was laid to rest by the same hands he taught to kill. There was no vengeance for his murder, no trial, no persecution.

Marcus even showed up to the funeral. Everyone thought that there was about to be a war as Marcus approached Tre who was still weeping at the gravesite. Instead, he pulled his brother up and hugged him, apologizing profusely for his wrongdoing.

"I'm sorry, bro," I heard him whisper to Tre.

Tre just hugged him back. They needed each other in that moment. Even after all of the commotion, it felt right. All felt right with the world. Everyone had come together including Simone and

Kalief. She had survived her own war and wanted to come out and pay her respects to a fallen soldier.

"Hi, boo, I'm so glad you're all right," she said, hugging me tightly.

"Same to you. You have no idea how bad I felt not being there for you after what happened."

I went missing right after the fiasco at her wedding. That weighed heavily on my chest because the whole time, I had to live with the grief of not knowing if she made it. She did, though, and that was the best news I had received in forever.

Kia and Rico were there and looked to be happy. I didn't know if they were there for show or fasho, but they were there and that made me happy.

Chase and Isabella had arrived and brought Lola along. This wasn't a time for smiles, but I couldn't help but cheese when I saw that big rock on her finger. The crew was still strong, and we were all here, no matter what.

THE END

This is book #4 and I seriously can't believe I mustered up the strength to complete it. There were times when I wanted to give up because the depression outweighed the passion. I sought help and I encourage anyone who may be dealing with a mental illness to seek help as well. Therapists are your friend and if they can help me, I know they can help anybody. Society makes us feel like we are crazy for being able to identify that something may be wrong. Don't ever let anyone convince that you shouldn't seek help.

There will be many more exciting books dropping from me this year, so be on the lookout! Thank you again for the support and for waiting patiently for this release. I love you guys.

Facebook: Author Santana, Jasmine Jones

Instagram: Author Santana

Twitter: @authorsantana

Catalogue:

She Was A Thug's Weakness: http://a.co/h4E11cP

The Other Side Of A Thug: http://a.co/6NDVLc

Womanizer: http://a.co/4EnFloL

Made in the USA
Monee, IL
14 July 2022